Brock

Hathaway House, Book 2

Dale Mayer

Books in This Series:

BROCK: HATHAWAY HOUSE, BOOK 2
Dale Mayer
Valley Publishing Ltd.

Copyright © 2019

ISBN-13: 978-1-773361-51-2
Print Edition

About This Book

Welcome to Hathaway House, a heartwarming military romance series from USA TODAY best-selling author Dale Mayer. Here you'll meet a whole new group of friends, along with a few favorite characters from Heroes for Hire. Instead of action, you'll find emotion. Instead of suspense, you'll find healing. Instead of romance, ... oh, wait. ... There is romance—of course!

Welcome to Hathaway House. Rehab Center. Safe Haven. Second chance at life and love.

Former Navy SEAL Brock Gorman has been at Hathaway House for more than a month with minimal improvement to either his physical or mental health. An vehicle accident on base two months ago caused major hip, back, and shoulder injuries that and took away any chance he had of ever going on a mission again. Making it through BUD/S training and into the SEALs teams was the crowning glory of Brock's life. Now it's gone. Why try to get better when he has nothing left to live for?

Physiotherapist Sidney Morning has been away from Hathaway House for nine months of specialized training. When she returns, there's Brock. And, while she loves the tough cases, he might be more than she can handle. He's big. He's strong. He's stubborn. He's gorgeous. And he's not making the efforts needed to get better. But, if Sidney can get under his skin and force him to jumping hurdles he's not interested in jumping, she can help him see that there are things which still make life worth living.

Sparks fly as Sidney and Brock fight their own emotions and each other, pushing Brock where he needs to go. ... If they are lucky, he might find both healing and love at Hathaway House.

Sign up to be notified of all Dale's releases here!
https://smarturl.it/DaleNews

Prologue

DANI WALKED TO where Aaron sat on the fence. He still couldn't believe they were together. She was so damn special. And he'd been such a heel... Still he was strong and fit and looking forward to a future with her and hopefully going to veterinarian school.

He looked up and smiled, accepting the mug. "Midnight is enjoying being around the little one."

"Midnight loves everyone," she said with a chuckle. Then held out two pieces of mail.

He took a sip as he eyed the bigger envelope, from the DOD. He flashed it to her, and she nodded, patting his cheek this time. He opened it to find a licensing contract for his patent on Helga's special prosthesis. He showed Dani. "Sweetheart, I'm getting paid!"

She gasped and tried to focus on the document Aaron waved before her.

"I'm so proud of you, Aaron." She snuggled closer to him, dropping a kiss on his lips.

Then he saw the small number ten envelope with the navy's return address. He ripped it open, found the check and was speechless.

Dani raised her head. "What is it, honey?"

He held it before her eyes.

"Oh, my God."

He nodded. Looked at it again before he faced her. "I know exactly what to do with this. I want to use some of it for someone with no insurance or donation help to come to the center."

Tears came to Dani's eyes as she heard those words.

"And I want to choose who gets it. You've got four coming in a few days, right?"

She nodded, too choked up to speak.

"Any pro bono cases?"

"Yes, two," she said with a sniffle.

He smiled at her and kissed her forehead. "I'll let you know which one then." He waited as she reached for a tissue and blew her nose. "And one final piece of news."

She checked his hands, probably looking for more mail. Instead she saw the small jeweler's box. And gasped.

"Dani Hathaway," Aaron said, "you've been here for me during the worst of my days—and my out-of-control temper and ego. Now I want to spend the best of my days with you. Will you marry me?"

She was full-on crying now, hugging him close, trying to breathe through her mouth. And she was the most precious thing he had seen in his life. "Will you marry me, Dani?" he asked again.

She nodded, sniffling. "I've been waiting for you for most of my life."

THE FOUR NEWEST rehab patients arrived several weeks later, and Aaron and Dani—still staring at her engagement ring—were there to meet them. Along with George, Shane, Dr. Herzog, the major, plus Helga, Racer, Tipler, Maggie and Molly. And so many more …

"Welcome to the Hathaway House," Aaron said, his arms spread wide. "We are all here to help in your healing and recovery. Yes even me…"

The four injured men seemed as dazed as Aaron probably was on his first day here. Then the three friends Dani was hoping to have in at the same time hadn't happened. Only one was here. But it was the one he knew. He perused the four and found him.

The first guy asked, "Where are we?"

"Texas," Aaron said with a smile.

The second guy took a 360-degree turn in his wheelchair, a blanket covering his lap but not hiding the fact he was missing a leg. He checked things out with a disapproving frown firmly in place. "You can't possibly know what I'm going through," he nearly growled.

Aaron raised his pant leg to show off his newest prosthesis. "Designed by yours truly."

The third guy was all stoic machismo silence, his one arm crossed tightly over his chest.

But it was the fourth man who asked, "What the hell is this place?"

Aaron whispered to Dani, "That's Brock. He's my guy." Then Aaron stepped forward to address all the newcomers as the words he was given on his first day came back to him. "Right now you hate this place. You want to be anywhere else but here. However, in a couple weeks, you'll never want to be anywhere else." He studied the men in front of him. "Are you ready?"

BROCK ONLY HALF listened to the conversation as he studied the man in front of him. A different man from the one he knew. Then major trauma changed a person. He didn't know the first thing about this place. And maybe that was a good thing. Maybe—if they also didn't know about him— he could start fresh.

Brock knew Aaron. Not well like many others he knew, but Aaron was a good man. A solid fighter and someone Brock could trust. If Aaron had done okay here, then maybe ... And if that was the case then the rest of Brock's unit could also come. Cole, Denton, Elliot—had all been injured in a mission after Brock had been hospitalized. Brock knew Elliot the best. But doubted he'd like Hathaway House. Not his style.

Then again, Brock's unit had all changed. Who knew what lay ahead of them? What he did know was there was no going back. This was his life now—no matter how he felt about it. So far it had been ugly as sin.

He waited a moment, then gave a decisive nod. "Let's do it."

Chapter 1

SIDNEY MORNING WALKED into Hathaway House and smiled. Nine months was a long time to be away, and she was happy to be home.

She spotted Dani, the owner and manager of Hathaway, behind the front desk and made her way over. Why she was working the desk was anyone's guess, but knowing Dani, it was because somebody else had had to step away, so she'd stepped in. Dani was like that. But clearly, she needed to hire more staff to handle the administrative side.

Dani finally lifted her face and looked at her a moment, her gaze confused, before she suddenly lit up. She bounded to her feet, came quickly around the counter and threw her arms around her.

"Oh, my goodness, Sidney! You're back!"

Sidney fiercely returned the hug. That was another reason she was happy to come back. These people were her family. She didn't have many blood relatives, and the ones she did have didn't remember her, anyway. That was the sad truth of Alzheimer's. Her mom had early onset, and even though she was only in her late fifties, she had no clue who Sidney was when Sidney visited her. It just made the visits harder and more bittersweet. There was a part of Sidney that said she didn't need to bother going because her mom didn't know who she was, but then she realized there was nobody else to make sure her mom was getting the care she needed, and that if Sidney didn't keep an eye out for her, anything could happen, and nobody would be the wiser. That couldn't be allowed to happen. She loved her mom. The memory of the woman she had been couldn't be allowed to be forgotten.

She stepped back from Dani's hug and smiled. "It's so good to be back. What's different?" She leaned forward and peered into Dani's brimming eyes. Tears? But happy ones, by the looks of things. Sidney glanced around the entry and reception area, but everything appeared to be the same. She shook her head and turned back to Dani. "Okay, give. What happened while I was gone?"

Dani beamed. "One of the nicest things that could possibly happen," she said in a low voice. She glanced behind her. "I met someone." She shrugged. "He's everything I could've hoped for." Then she added, "And, I broke my own rule ... he was a patient here."

Sidney's eyebrows shot up to her hairline. Not only was that something Dani had firmly said was against the rules, but many of the people here for treatment were not in the right frame of mind for a relationship. Therefore, she was hesitant in her optimism for her friend's sake. "What kind of shape is he in?"

Dani grinned. "He lost a leg in the accident that sent him here and has some damage to his back."

"And mentally?" Sidney asked bluntly. She'd never been one to hold back, and she wasn't about to start now. Sure as hell, anybody who respected and cared about Dani wasn't going to either.

"He's in a good place. I'm certain of that."

"Okay. Have you had any word from the asshole, since?"

"No," Dani said, her voice tinged with relief. "None."

"Good." Sidney had been the second one to find Dani after her last boyfriend had beat the crap out of her. She hoped to never see such a thing again, especially not when it was somebody as nice and genuine as Dani. She gave her friend an optimistic smile and said, "Well, then, I look forward to meeting this new guy."

"I want you to meet him, too," Dani replied happily. "He's visiting his brother right now but should be back in a few weeks."

Sidney glanced down at the room chart, which was open on the other side of the reception desk, and asked, "How full are we right now?"

"Full," Dani said with a heavy sigh. "Aaron moved into the house with me so we could use his room," she said blushing. "I'm really glad to have you back. We have a couple of people coming back in, looking for short-term assistance on top of a full house."

"That's unusual," Sidney said. "Of course, that means business is booming, and that's a good thing for the center but sad for the state of the world." She glanced outside to the fields surrounding the center. "The animals?"

"Well, that's increasing, too. Stan is taking on an assistant, and they're going to be doing more surgeries downstairs," Dani said with a smile. "Aaron, my fiancé, is actually finishing his schooling to become a vet."

Sidney's eyebrows popped again. Then she grinned. "Sounds like you just might like him because he can help you make the center bigger and better."

The two women chuckled. "Not likely," Dani scoffed. "Although he's helped out a ton at the center too. Been great at getting some of the new arrivals settled in. What about you, are you settled in?"

"I am. I got in late last night and headed straight to my room. I'm glad it's still there," she teased.

Dani shook her head. "I'll tell you, it was close. We were getting to the point I was tempted to set it up as a patient room."

"Yeah, but you know I always come back," Sidney said with a smile. "Is my roster full?" It was one of the things Sidney loved most about Dani and Hathaway. Employees were strongly encouraged to continue training and education when possible—and jobs were always waiting when they came back.

"Oh, is it ever!"

"You know I like the toughest ones," Sidney said with spirit. In fact, she really did prefer them that way. She was a very warm-hearted, compassionate person, but she had no compunction about pushing these men and women into doing what they had to do, especially when they needed it.

"Well, you get to start with Brock," Dani said with a groan. "He's pretty well worn everybody else out."

"What's his problem?"

"He was injured in a car accident at work, but on US soil, and he hates the fact he wasn't injured while fighting. He's done two tours in Afghanistan and one tour in Iraq and then he came home and got in a crappy car accident, which has caused all kinds of hip, back and arm problems."

"And of course, psychologically, he feels guilty and stupid."

Dani sent her a sharp look. "He's not very open to talking about it. He's big. He's strong. He came here voluntarily, as his progress had stalled, and he did better, but then almost immediately, he's plateaued."

"Lead on, Macduff. I'll see how we get along."

"Actually, I just assumed there was no getting along. You need to go in and take charge. He's pretty much sent everybody else out of there in tears."

"Oh, good. He's perfect for me then because I'm ripe and ready to get back into some butt-kicking. He won't be sending me out in tears."

It wasn't that Sidney thought she was beyond breaking down over a patient, because she definitely wasn't, but she'd do it in a different time and place and certainly not where they could see it. If he was badgering, or in any way being hostile, well, that would just get her back up.

"Do you want to meet him first or see his file?"

"I want to meet him."

Dani sent her a conspiratorial smile and said, "Let's go."

They walked down the hallway, took a left and headed down around the corner.

"He's got one of the last rooms on this side?" asked Sidney.

"Yes." Dani nodded. "He's a very heavy snorer. The patients here have enough trouble sleeping without that on top of everything else, so we had to move him down here."

"Nasal cavity issues?"

"Yes, and he sleeps on his back. It's not his choice, but with his injuries it's about the only way he can knock himself out. He doesn't sleep well."

It was often a problem with those types of injuries. People had favorite sleeping positions, but after major trauma it was often not possible to lie in that position again. Their balance shifted, affecting natural pressure points. Everything changed, and sleep often suffered. She'd have to see if that was one of the things they could get Brock to improve. A good night's sleep was worth its weight in gold.

Dani rapped smartly on the door of the last room. A growl, and then a sigh, came from inside.

Sidney heard him and snickered. It was just way too cliché. She followed Dani into the room to see a big bear of a man lying fully-dressed across his bed with a laptop across his thighs. He raised his gaze, nodded to Dani, and then looked at Sidney and frowned. She frowned right back at him.

Like hell she was going to force him into doing anything she wanted. He was going to do it because he was here, and that was what he came for.

"Good morning, Brock. This is Sidney Morning. She was away, upgrading her training and thankfully she's back again," Dani said with a smile. "She will be taking over your physiotherapy."

Brock's frown deepened. "She doesn't look strong enough to do anything. And why the upgrading? Is she not fully certified?"

"Looks can be deceiving, because clearly, you look like you should be strong enough to do everything asked of you, but you're not," Sidney retorted.

She heard Dani suck in her breath in shock. But there was no way in hell she was backing down. Brock's eyebrows rose, and the look in his eyes turned from a steely glare to a hardened glint. She smiled at him. "Now we understand each other perfectly. I'll go grab your file, update myself on how far you've gotten and I'll be back in about twenty minutes."

With that, Sidney turned and walked out. She waited for Dani in the hallway and overheard an exchange in the room.

"Sidney is one of the best physiotherapists there is," Dani said.

"Does that mean she's allowed to have a lousy bedside manner?" Brock's voice was a grumble.

Sidney snickered out loud at that. Inside, she was revved up and ready to go. She rubbed her hands together gleefully. This was going to be fun.

Dani joined her and shook her head at the big grin on Sidney's face. "You really want to do it this way?"

"Oh, yeah. We'll see how he's doing in a couple of weeks."

"Okay, if you're positive. Let's get a cup of coffee, and I'll get his file and all the others for you."

The two walked through the cafeteria where lots of people sang out greetings to Sidney. She'd always loved the people here, and they seemed to love her in return. As a homecoming, it was perfect.

They got their coffees and headed back toward Dani's office.

Once inside, Sidney sat down in the visitor's chair. "I'm really glad to be back."

Dani smiled, picking up a stack of files, including a very thick one on top, and handed it to her. "I'm really glad to have you back." She nodded at the top folder and added, "And not just because of Brock."

"You have others like him?" Sidney laughed. "Sounds like I returned just in time."

"You know normally we only have one this difficult at a time." Dani groaned. "He's the most difficult, but there are a few others that need a little something extra." She smiled at Sidney. "You have that something extra."

"I'm just me."

"That means you are just perfect for here."

BROCK STARED AT the empty doorway. He wasn't sure what to think of the new therapist. There hadn't been anything wrong with any of the others. But he certainly hadn't been motivated to do his best or give his deepest efforts. He knew there was something wrong inside him, but he'd given acting normal a good shot. He'd thought he had them fooled but apparently not.

Or they were bluffing.

Instantly, he tossed that idea out. They were all professionals here. He'd seen it over and over again. It was really himself he was trying to fool. But why? He stared down at his big hands. His big mitts. That was what his sister had always called them. He supposed they were, especially when compared to her small, long, slender fingers. But his mitts were meant for hard, physical work. Shovels fit perfectly in his hands, as did hammers and saws and any other kind of tool, but especially weapons. He'd always reveled in his physical strength—his ability to do the hard work. So many hated it, but he loved it. His body rejoiced in using his muscles, using his strength. He'd grown fast and tall and hadn't really been aware he was the tallest in the family and still growing. Then, he'd started to fill out. While he was in high school, he'd taken on several part-time jobs. Roofing was one of them, and that was because he loved carrying the big packs of tiles around the roofs. If he did nothing else but carry them up and down all day long, he was content.

His appointment to the military had been perfect for him. He'd reveled in the physical training, and he'd excelled at the mental discipline. It had been a really good fit until his accident. But now he was no longer active. They might be able to find a job for him at a desk, or in some supply office, but how did one go from being the best of the best to being ... almost nothing at all?

He certainly didn't want to mock those not in the navy. It wasn't for everyone. But it was for him.

As for him, a desk job would kill him. It wasn't what he wanted to do—it wasn't what he could do, and it wasn't what he should do.

But his active military lifestyle was over. The phone call had finished it. He shook his head, staring out the window. He had been doing fine until that. It wasn't that he had felt self-pity, or had self-doubt, it was more about apathy. A lack of caring. It was like his wellness was over, so now, who gave a damn? Like he wanted to beg for a tour in Iraq he would just not come home from. Surely that would be better than the slow wasting away here.

He'd spoken with his counselor several times, but he hadn't managed to tell him about the phone call shutting down his last avenue in the military. There would be such finality if he actually verbalized it. While nobody knew, it seemed like it wasn't real. There was hope of something changing it. But of course, he was only fooling himself.

Besides, the counselor had mentioned antidepressants earlier as well. That was the last thing he wanted. That was just going to put a pretty mask on a sad situation. It was nothing he couldn't handle, but he wanted to solve the problem—permanently. That meant finding another purpose in life. He couldn't go back to the straight physical work he had been doing. And he was nowhere as young as he had once been. He was thirty-three—the navy had been the best of the best in all things. He'd been a SEAL. Achieving that status had been a crowning glory of his life. Now, it was over. He'd had six good years there. At thirty-three he hadn't been ready to leave. But life—and the brass—had decided otherwise.

It wasn't that he was fighting his physiotherapy, because he wasn't, but neither was he actively working toward his recovery. In high school, one of the classes they'd been forced to take was several weeks' worth of meditation. Now, the world was so stressful if he could relearn the basics, maybe it could help him get through this stage more easily. There had been one particular exercise that came back to him now. They had to imagine themselves in a cloud, completely surrounded by a white fog and unable see the ground or the sky. All they could see when they looked down was a few inches of tiling underneath their feet. The instructor had said they had to take a step forward. Brock had asked her how they could take a step forward when they had no idea what was ahead of them. She'd smiled and said that was the point of the exercise. One had to have faith.

He'd never managed to complete the exercise because he didn't have faith. Not in himself. He'd been raised without religion. A cocky young man who hadn't needed it. Faith was for other people. In time, he had understood. It wasn't so much about faith and religion, as it was about being able to trust. Trust that there was going to be something, or someone, there to catch him if he should fall. Trust that if his feet were standing on something solid he could find the next step he needed to take. And here he was, lying in bed again, trying to surround himself with that cloud. He needed to step forward, but because he couldn't see where he was going, he didn't know how to take that step. It was all because, of course, he had no faith, no trust that something would break his fall. He didn't even know if the direction he was going to choose was the one he wanted to be traveling in.

He knew there was something deeply personal in all of these musings. He had yet to find a truth that would help him navigate these troubled waters. He knew the new therapist was going to arrive soon, and he wasn't sure he was ready for her, either. She reminded him of one of his old military superiors. Someone so high and mighty he tried to force everybody to do his bidding just so he could feel all-powerful.

In the military, he saw all kinds of people. He had to work with all kinds of people. Maybe that was a good thing. He didn't need to do that anymore. He didn't have to take her attitude if he really disliked her. He could complain. Have one of the others again.

Yet, he'd accomplished little here so far. He had only pushed himself to a point. He had done what he was supposed to do, nothing more. He realized that as far as he was concerned, he was still standing in a cloud. If he pushed himself any harder, it was going to force him into the unknown. In which case ... what if he fell?

Chapter 2

S IDNEY STUDIED THE thick file in front of her. She was still sitting in Dani's office going over the material. There was a packet of X-rays in the back, too. She realized Brock had sustained more injuries than she'd expected. She frowned as she read the notes about the original damage. He'd been to hell and back. A wrenched back, several broken bones, ripped tendons and severed muscles. The damage extended from his central spine around to the side and even his hip flexors were a mess. She shook her head. "How long has he been here?"

"Four weeks," Dani said.

Sidney nodded. She flipped back to the beginning of the file to see the other therapy reports. He was a hard worker but only to the point he was pushed. He never gave any extra. It was like he was doing what he had to do, but no more. If they told him six feet, he made sure it was six feet, but he never did six feet and a quarter. And that wasn't good because it meant he wasn't engaged in his own healing.

She sifted through the papers, looking for the psychologist's report, and studied several of the notations on it. He had his own file he kept on every patient, but when it was necessary for the team to understand what was going on, he'd add notes to the generic case file.

Sidney didn't want to have to point out these revelations

to Brock. That wouldn't help him heal as much as if he figured it out himself. That was what this place was about—healing on all levels. Being told what to do, and actively engaging in doing what needed to be done, were two different things.

She stood with his file in her hand and said, "I'll go talk to Brock now."

Dani looked up and nodded. "Take it easy on him. He's had a rough couple of nights. Nightmares again. He hasn't been able to tell anybody about them yet. That will happen over time."

"It would be good to know if there was a specific trigger for their return." Sidney held up the file. "Not that nightmares need a trigger. They sit in our subconscious ready to rise at any moment."

"You can always ask if you find the right moment. Maybe you can get it out of him." Dani gave her a bright smile. "If anybody can, you can."

Sidney shook her head with a laugh. "Such confidence."

"And well placed."

With a last glance at Dani, Sidney walked out and headed toward Brock. It was now nine-thirty in the morning. Hopefully, he was up and doing something active. It was up to her to get him moving. She knew he wasn't going to want to be tested, to be pushed, to see how far he could go. There might be an easier way to figure out why he was holding back. She'd read every note and understood the others' take on it, but she was coming at the problem from a slightly different angle. She specialized in these big guys. They were all stubborn, but they usually had huge hearts. When they shut that down it was like everything else stopped working. If their heart wasn't in it, nothing was going to move.

She stopped at his doorway and studied him. She couldn't help the pang of disappointment to see he was still lying on the bed. At least he was fully dressed. He was ambulatory, unlike so many others at the center. He could walk on his own somewhat, with the help of crutches to ease the pain in his back. But right now he was doing nothing but staring out the window. His fists clenched repeatedly in a rhythmic movement. She didn't think he was deliberately trying to do an exercise—rather, it was emotion driving them.

She plastered a bright smile on her face, rapped sharply on the door and walked in.

"Okay, I'm back. I've got this monster of a file here, and I've flicked through some of it, but obviously, I don't have time to read it all at the moment. I will later. What I do want you to do is tell me one of the aspects you like about the physio you've done so far and which part of it you don't like."

Instead of sitting in a chair beside him she sat down on the end of his bed. He didn't shift his legs to give her more space, just stared at her with that deep, dark gaze.

As she studied him she saw the first sign of the emotional weakness. Grief.

Seeing that, she changed her approach. She went from domineering and powerful to something gentler. She didn't understand what was going on inside him, but there was something so dramatic that it had worked its way through every part of his psyche. They were going to have to get to the root of that, but she couldn't do it without him trusting her.

"It's important to discuss what you like and what you don't like, so we can work together on a program that you will push yourself on." She kept her voice neutral and in control. She studied his gaze, but it had switched back to looking out the window. "I certainly have a program we can start with, if you prefer."

Again, no answer. She bounced to her feet and said, "Or, I can be a hard-ass."

Her reward for that was a tiny sniff.

She grinned. "I guess you don't believe me."

At that, his gaze shifted back to look at her. His eyes swept her from her toes and back up again.

"You're about a hundred and fifty pounds, nowhere near my 'mean.' For all your talk, you're a marshmallow on the inside," he said. "I've been brutalized by the best. Go ahead and do your worst."

"I don't have any intention of trying to force you into a wheelchair or into doing exercises. That's not what I'm here for. I'd rather spend my time with somebody who is trying than waste it trying to get somebody to give a damn. I thought you were a former SEAL. All-in, all the time. But I guess not. You're just dead weight." She stepped forward and put herself into his line of vision. "If you don't want to be here, I'm sure we can get you the hell out." She looked down at her watch and said, "I'll be back in an hour. You make your decision. You're either in that wheelchair, ready to get down to the exercise room, or I'll tell Dani you're looking for a transfer out."

Without waiting for an answer, she turned and walked out. Like hell she was going to deal with that shit. He was either in here or he was out, but she needed to know right from the beginning. As she went down the hallway she meekly pinched the bridge of her nose and realized how quickly he had gotten to her. She could see why Dani was happy to have her back. She'd had several other difficult patients before, and they'd often refused to do very much. This wasn't a holiday. His bed was needed for somebody who wanted to have an active part in their own healing and recovery.

She poked her head into Dani's office. "I'm still standing."

Dani chuckled. "Didn't get too far the first time?"

"Actually, I told him that if he wasn't going to be taking part in getting into his wheelchair and getting ready to go do what we needed to do, then I'd tell you that you needed to do a transfer."

"If he wants to transfer out," Dani said, leaning back in her chair, her expression thoughtful, "then of course, he can do that."

"Then can you start looking into that?" Sidney replied.

Sidney walked out of Dani's office with heavy sigh. She understood they wanted everyone here to do well, but Sidney was more of the opinion they needed to help those who were ready to help themselves. This wasn't a rest home for those who wanted to retire from living. She walked out onto the deck and grabbed a cup of coffee. Yet another that she probably didn't need. Then she caught sight of the Major. She had no idea if Dani's father had officially obtained that rank, or if it had been tossed onto his shoulders as a joke at some point, but it just stuck. His face lit up when he saw her, and he opened his arms.

She put her coffee cup down on the closest table and hugged him.

"Oh, my goodness, it's so good to see you," she said with a big smile. And indeed, it was. He was brimming with health and vitality. "I can see you haven't had a bad day since

I left," she said in admiration. "You're looking very fit and relaxed."

"Doctor's orders," he said with a big grin. "Now that Dani is happily together with Aaron I can relax a little bit."

Sidney laughed. "Is this a temporary situation, or do you really think this is it?"

He lost some of his humor, and instead she saw a deeper satisfaction in his gaze. "You know, I think they just might make it. Aaron is a good man and more than that, now that he's got his own health back, he cares about others. Those here and those that want to come ... He's a huge asset to both the center and a great partner for Dani."

"Then I'm jealous," Sidney announced. "Wish we could all be so lucky."

"Stick around here. I'm sure you'll find somebody to love." He nodded behind him and said, "There are a lot of men here looking for a good woman."

Sidney shook her head and smiled. "But that's against the rules, you know."

The Major waved a hand in the air dismissively. "Pshaw. Rules are sometimes meant to be broken. People are always looking for love."

"Most of the men here are looking for new lives. They'll take them any way they can get them, and that doesn't necessarily include love."

He chuckled. "Bring your coffee over my way and sit for a minute," he said, motioning to a table out in the sunshine. "Bring me up to speed. How was the course?"

She took her coffee and joined him. The Major had always been interested in everybody in this place. When Sidney finally checked her watch, she saw she'd been there longer than twenty minutes.

"You have to be someplace?" the Major asked in surprise. "Are you working already today?"

"Absolutely. Dani's a slave driver." They grinned at each other, because, of course, it was just the opposite. In many ways, Dani was too easygoing, but she had people working for her that were independent, self-motivated and driven. They didn't need mothering. They just needed to be let loose to do their thing. Sidney could count herself at the top of that list. Suddenly, her phone rang. She clicked on it to see Shane's name.

"Hello?"

"Hey, girl, I heard you just got back, but it's not like you to be late."

"Late?" She didn't have a place to go. "I have no place to be late for."

"Your patient's here. He's already set up on the weights."

"Brock?" she asked slowly. "Is that who you're talking about?"

"You got it. He's been here a while, and we don't seem to get along too well. So, you may just want to come down here and help us out."

She knew he was only half joking. They were professionals, and everybody did the job they had to do. But like in any small community, there were those they got along with better than others. Brock had made a point of not getting along with anybody.

Nobody liked to carry dead weight.

"I'll be down in a few minutes."

She smiled at the Major and patted his hand. "Duty calls."

She put her dirty cup and saucer in the appropriate rack and contemplated what the news meant. Obviously Brock wasn't looking for a transfer. She wondered if she should tell Dani or wait until later. She decided later was probably a better idea. As she walked into the physio room, Shane gave her a high five and walked out. She hadn't exactly planned on starting here, but she took it to mean Brock preferred working on the weights. Then, of course, he was a big, strapping man, and likely used to having a big, fit body. This was going to be an important part of recovery. She could use that. Wanting ... no, needing to get that power back, that sense of completeness, that sense of self was what this was all about. Sure, they were going to work on the injuries, and they would heal and strengthen every ounce of him they could. Mobility was high on that list as well. But all of it would come together much faster if he could ease back and be happy with who he was. He had expectations. *They* had expectations. But rarely did they ever go together. It was so important to be able to communicate and find that middle ground.

She dug up that bright smile again and walked over to him. "Now, this is a good place to start. Let's see if we can get that awesome body back."

He looked up at her and frowned. "I'm never going to get that back."

"You might not with Shane, there. But you will with me, if you're ready to do the work."

For the first time, she saw a hint of interest in his gaze. Good, she'd been right about that. She'd worked with several bodybuilders in her time. She knew how important it was for them to have that look, or maybe that feel. She didn't think he was bodybuilding material, a strongman competition would be better, but he'd been in incredibly good shape. So, he knew exactly what was required to maintain it. He was a long way away from that point. It was going be hard on him, but she could help him make a comeback—at least as much of one as he was ready to have.

SIDNEY WAS NOT at all what he had expected. She'd come off as such a hard-ass this morning. Some of what she'd said burned. And some rang with truth. He didn't want to transfer away, so here he was. And here she was, capable of seeing what he wanted out of this and trying to help him get it. He wasn't concerned about appearances, but he knew damned well that having a strong back was going to make a difference in his work life. That was what he wanted. He wanted to feel like he could do everyday tasks and chores with at least a certain amount of ability.

It meant a hell of a lot of muscle repair. He was up for it as long as the end result was the same goal he wanted. He wasn't even sure why he hadn't been able to work with the others. It wasn't that they hadn't wanted to help him because they had. Nor had they not seen that he needed help because they certainly had, and they were definitely professionals. But there'd been just something about doing the endless number of exercises, listening to them drone on and on about the body's muscle groups and the injuries that made him want to throw the weights across the room.

One thing he did know. He didn't want to leave Hathaway. So far, this seemed like it was the best place for him. He just needed somebody to help him get where he needed to be. Maybe his luck had finally changed—maybe she was going to be the one.

Two hours later, he was cursing her out—and she was

cursing right back at him.

"Come on. Push your sorry ass into that move. Don't you start wussing out on me, you little weasel." She danced in front of him as he pushed and tugged and pulled—moving the muscles, building the muscles, toning the injuries and forcing them to heal.

He glared at her and swore. "Don't take your frustrations out on me, you bitch."

She grinned. "Call me any name in the book. I don't care. You're not going to send me running. Besides, it just shows your lack of control."

"Goddammit," he roared and did one more set.

She laughed. "Now that's what I'm talking about."

"I'm so not happy with you right now." Sweat dripped, burning into his eyes. His body bowed over the weights and his back ... Jesus! He hurt.

"No, but you can put that big mouth of yours into the job and make the next move."

And on it went. By the time he was done, he was afraid he really was done. He'd never been so goddamned sore in all his life. All those knots of the last six months, and the months of lying in bed, the workouts up until now—all of it had been nothing. He sat down with a sigh, realizing his whole body was trembling.

With any luck this torture was over—at least for the moment. However, he was quietly amazed. He had no idea that was inside of him. After completing BUD/s training, he'd felt invincible. The best of the best. He'd had a sense of personal accomplishment that had been the highlight of his life.

Now, all he wanted to do was make his way back to bed and stay there, pampering himself with room service and forgetting about getting out of bed again—ever.

Sidney had different ideas. With a sneer, she said, "Look at you, you're already finished. Down to the pool! Twenty laps, and then we'll consider a massage."

Shit. He glared at her in outrage. Had she read his chart? Did she know what he used to do? That swimming was a major part of a Navy SEALs career? Did she even care? "Twenty laps? Maybe I can't even swim," he challenged her. "Did you even think about that?"

She shoved her face in his and said, "Then it should be an easy walk on the pool bottom, Tank."

He stared at her for a few minutes, and then he howled. Not at just being called a tank, but at the image of him walking on the floor of the pool. He'd actually been really good at that when he was a kid.

Spirits high, and too tired to walk, he sat himself down in the wheelchair and headed for the elevator.

This might just work out after all.

Chapter 3

B Y THE TIME he'd made it through the pool session, she wondered if she'd overdone it. He was looking a little on the shaky side. However, his jaw was stiff, as if he was clenching it and refusing to break down and tell her. She could believe he'd had some of the worst taskmasters in the world. The military wasn't known for light, fluffy workouts. At the same time, she didn't want to be put in the same category. He did need to work, but he couldn't afford to overdo it. Strain injuries were way too common in this business. By the time she'd helped him sit down on the bench, he'd relaxed slightly. She grabbed some towels.

"Do you want your massage down here or back up in your room?"

His answer was telling. "My bed, please."

"Wheelchair or walk?"

Silence. He looked at the wheelchair, looked over at her and then stood. Instantly, he wavered. She moved the wheelchair into position behind him and pressed him back to sit down. "You can walk another time."

She didn't give him any chance to answer but wheeled him toward the elevator. Just because he was ambulatory didn't mean he was in the best position to make his way on foot all the time. Sometimes the workouts were just that much harder. Upstairs in his room, he was still dripping wet in his swimsuit, and she threw his dry towels down on the bed and wheeled him over to the side. She asked, "Do you need any help?"

She was fully expecting to walk out without doing anything more for him because she knew how stubborn he was.

There was fatigue in his voice when he answered, "Could you pull the bedding back?"

She could see the bedding had bundled up. She untangled it and folded it back. Then she took several towels and stretched them out on top of the bed. "You can put on dry trunks or lie down without any on," she said. "I'll be back in a few minutes."

With that, she walked out of the room. She headed into the office the physiotherapists shared where she had her own desk and dropped her towel on the back of the chair. She sat down, brought up his file on the computer and quickly updated it with the day's efforts. He'd done a hell of a job so far.

He was going to need a massage, however, to stop the muscles from tightening up too much.

She'd picked up a couple of really good creams while she'd been away this last time. Some had special ingredients to help make the muscles heal a little faster. When she was done at the computer, she went to her locker, found the cream she wanted and returned to his room. He was lying on his stomach without a pillow, completely flat, with his eyes closed. A towel lay across his backside. She could tell he had no trunks on. Good, she didn't want anything to impede her work. She opened up the cream, rubbed some on her hands and put the tube back onto the table. She kept the lid off in case she needed more. She hadn't worked on him before, so she had no idea how dry his skin was.

She started on the big trapezius muscles, gently at first. Mentally, she tested the tightness, the muscle mass from the injuries and his pain tolerance levels.

"You can go a lot harder than that," he murmured.

"All in good time," she said.

Every therapist she knew had their own individual system. She liked to work lightly to loosen and warm up the muscles. Then, she dug deeper and deeper, working at the knots, working at the tension, trying to ease everything up so the muscles relaxed. Staying focused, she worked her way through his back, his upper arms, shoulders and neck. Then she slowly worked down toward the bed of scars on the left side. She'd seen a lot of injuries in her life. Particularly working here, but these were some of the largest expanses of soft-tissue injury she'd ever seen.

Compassion filled her as she gently eased back the pressure where the muscle layer thinned down. His recovery would have been painful as hell. As soon as she touched the area above his hip, she could feel him tensing up again. With one hand working the top of his neck, helping him to relax, she gently worked through the hip into the lower back. He was missing so much muscle development on that side it was almost painful for her to massage. She worked the whole area, refusing to give in to his pain, or her own, and then she slowly moved down. She pulled the towel off slightly to see part of his glutes had also been damaged. One side of his cheek was deformed. She grabbed some more cream, smearing it over her hands.

"Not very pretty, is it?" he said in a gritty voice.

"Pretty is not the issue," she said calmly. "It must be a pain in the ass not to be able to sit flush."

That startled a laugh out of him. "I hadn't actually noticed that being an issue."

"Good. Let's see if we can build those muscles up, at least enough that you won't sit lopsided." With that, she went back to work. By the time she was done and easing her hands up and down his spine and neck once again, she could feel his breath dropping into a smooth, calm, heavy breathing instead of being tense and waiting for more pain.

As she stepped away and pulled the blankets on top of him, she smiled.

He'd nodded off to sleep. She stooped and picked up the wet towels he'd dropped on the floor and tossed them into the laundry basket. She grabbed her cream and walked out. As she left, she flicked the light switch off and closed the door. She didn't want him to sleep too long because lunch was coming up. However, if anybody deserved a nap, it was him. As she headed back to the office she caught sight of Dani.

The other woman changed course and headed toward her. "How was it?"

"Well, I don't think you'll have to find a transfer for him," Sidney said with a big smile. "He's asleep right now. He worked hard—he deserves the rest."

Dani's shoulders slumped with relief, and a big smile flashed across her face. "Oh, my God, I'm so happy to hear that. He's such a good guy, but he just wasn't getting anywhere."

"Sometimes just changing the personalities is enough," Sidney said with another smile. She patted Dani on the shoulder. "Have you got time for lunch today?"

Dani glanced at her watch. "Sure. Let's go and eat."

Back in the dining room, there was another round of greetings from people who were seeing her for the first time since her return. Sidney picked up a Caesar salad, a sandwich, and a big yogurt, and carried the tray out onto the deck. Feeling welcomed and happy to be home again, she sat down and relaxed.

While she waited for Dani to join her, Sidney flexed her fingers, feeling the ache of a job well done. That was another issue she was potentially going to have to look at down the road. Often, massage therapists had to change careers by the time they were forty because of their own physical injuries—arthritis being one of the biggest. She was licensed in both physio and massage.

"Sore?" Dani asked as she sat down. Her tray was full with salmon, soup and a salad.

Sidney laughed wryly. "Yes. But I worked hard this morning." She leaned toward Dani and added in a conspiratorial voice, "Not as hard as he did, though."

With that, they both grinned and dug into their food, enjoying the conversation and just being back together again.

"You know," Sidney said, "as much as I really like this place, it was the animals I missed the most."

"The animals are both good and bad," Dani said. "We have a few easy cases—several needed to be spayed or neutered, and that's something we subsidize for the rescue shelter. Of course, Stan is also very interested in prosthetics for the animals, so he has a couple of people working there helping him out, too. Aaron has expressed interest in that field as well." She nodded toward a young horse in the field beside an older one.

"Her name's Molly. She came here with a badly cracked hoof. She'd actually been living in the owner's house as a pet." Dani shook her head. "The owner seemed to think she was going to end up as a dwarf of some kind. But instead, she's got a full-sized lineage."

Sidney laughed. "That must have come as quite a shock."

"When Molly came here, she had never met another horse. Now she's attached to Maggie, and the two of them are pretty much inseparable."

"Good. It's not like you're going to get rid of Maggie," Sidney said with a smile. "Molly is a very lucky filly. And speaking of lucky, tell me about Aaron," she added with a grin.

"As I mentioned earlier, Aaron is going to school to become a vet. Stan gave him an awesome referral, but he worked damn hard and got great grades on the courses he needed to pick up. He's planning to come back and work here." Dani lowered her voice, looking around to make sure nobody was listening. "It was pretty hard not to fall in love with him at that point."

Sidney laughed.

"And you? Whatever happened to John?"

Sidney had been waiting for that question, but now that it was here, she really didn't have an answer. "Nothing. That's the problem," she said with a sigh. "He didn't want to move forward because he didn't care enough."

"Ouch."

Sidney looked up to see Dani staring at her. She dropped her gaze to her food, unable to speak.

A moment later, Dani reached across the table and covered her hand with hers. "I'm so sorry. You're better off without him."

"I know that, but ..." Sidney glanced around at the very large seating area.

Dani had turned this place into a multi-functional, multi-purpose room that worked so well for everybody. Those who wanted to be inside could sit inside, and those who wanted to be outside could sit outside. There were large doors that could close in case of cooler, wet weather, but most of the time the weather here was perfect. There was a lot to be said for this part of Texas. She had had high hopes John might want to move here permanently, but apparently, permanency wasn't high on her ex's list of priorities.

Sidney shook her head. "It's been a while anyway. It happened when I first got back to class. I spent most of the term getting back on track again."

"Well, things have eased slightly here, by my own making." Dani gave her a gentle smile. "Not that I'm advocating matchmaking or anything."

"Oh, my God, no!" Sidney lowered her voice, glaring at her friend, who was grinning at her impishly. "Absolutely no way is that going to happen."

"Sure, I was just kidding." But her eyes didn't stop dancing.

Sidney stared at her in trepidation. "Just because you're so happy doesn't mean the rest the world has to be the same way," she cautioned. "I'm totally okay to not have any romance in my life for a while."

"I believe you." But then she snorted, letting Sidney know there was no way she believed her.

And Sidney knew that if Dani had a chance, she'd find somebody for Sidney.

Which was so *not* what she was looking for right now.

THE SUDDEN KNOCK woke Brock from his nap. He opened

his eyes, feeling disoriented. He was in his bed, covered up with a blanket. And he hurt. Oh God, he hurt. But it was a different kind of hurt. Not like after the first injury or the weeks he'd spent in hospital numbed with morphine. It was the type of hurt he used to feel. The burn after a hard workout where he knew his muscles were functioning like they were supposed to. The burn that spoke of tiny microfiber tears in his muscles before they could build up bigger, better and stronger. As he lay there, the memory of the morning flooded through him. Somehow, she had gotten him to work like he'd never worked before. He had to give her kudos for that. They had settled into a rhythm of swearing and cursing at each other, and somehow, he'd risen higher and higher and done more than he ever thought possible.

The hard knock came again. He let his head roll to the side and called out, "Come in."

He had to wonder at himself. Before his accident, he could never have imagined a point when he would lie in bed and let somebody come into his room. He would've hopped up and answered the door.

But now, he just couldn't be bothered. He also didn't know if it mattered. He'd changed in so many damned ways. The door opened and his doctor walked in, a frown crossing his face as he saw him.

"Are you sick, Brock?"

With a wry smile, Brock replied, "No, just tired."

Still frowning, the doctor clicked on his iPad and studied something on the screen.

Brock figured Sidney had updated the reports, so the doctor was likely reading them over. For some reason, he felt protective. He didn't want her to get in trouble. Not when she'd done so much good for him. He threw back the covers, deliberately keeping his face straight and not making a sound as he sat up. "I had a terrible night last night." He glanced at his watch. "It looks like I missed lunch."

"There's no such thing as missing lunch. Just tell one of the chefs to get you something. There are probably tons of leftovers anyway."

Brock nodded. The doctor was still studying his chart. He wanted to get up and walk to the door to find food, but he wasn't sure he could do it without making a sound. The first couple of steps were likely to be as painful as hell. But he hadn't been a SEAL for nothing. Gritting his teeth, he stood and slipped his foot into the slippers he wore at the center, only to realize he was nude. With sheer willpower, he dressed in shorts and a tank. Turning to the doctor, he said, "If you need to talk to me, come and have a coffee while I grab some food. But I need food right now."

And he walked out, leaving stunned silence behind him.

When he was in the hallway, he took a couple of deep breaths. He was amazed that with all the work he'd done this morning, he wasn't screaming in pain. He didn't look to see if the doctor was following him but continued on in a slow, steady walk—under his own steam. And wasn't that something?

He made it into the dining area in time to see the kitchen staff starting to put away the food. Tray in hand, he walked over to the buffet and served himself a large Caesar salad and fried chicken.

Dennis, who worked behind the counter, said, "If there is anything you need you can't find, just let us know. We're cleaning up and getting ready for dinner."

"I'll be fine with whatever's here," Brock said with a

smile. "It looks great." He made his way along the line and snagged a piece of apple pie. Finally, he added a coffee and turned to slowly look at the large room. There was a table between him and the hallway, and it was probably the easiest one for him to reach. He picked up the tray, and with careful, deliberate movements, he walked to the table and set the tray down. He could almost feel a sense of approval whisper throughout the room. He thought he was alone, but there were still a few stragglers.

As he sat down, a little too heavy, a little too hard for his own sense of comfort, he realized he'd actually made the trip on his own for the first time. No crutches or wheelchair. For many that would be nothing, but for him it was a huge accomplishment. He looked up, and his gaze landed on a group of his peers on the other side of the room, many of whom he knew at least by name. They smiled and nodded at him—he got a sense of approval all over again. It made him feel damned good, but embarrassed. He could feel the heat rising up his neck. He turned to stare down at the food in front of him, deliberately ignoring the discomfort. He didn't want to make a spectacle of himself, and he certainly didn't want to be on show, but if there was ever a time and place to put in a good effort, it'd been today.

Now, he was starved. He dove into his lunch and polished off the salad and chicken. By the time he got to the apple pie, he was starting to feel more human. Taking his time with the pie, coffee in hand, he stared out across the fields. In the weeks he'd been here, he had never yet made it to the animal center below. It seemed so weird when he first got here to think there was a full animal therapy center and veterinarian clinic below. It sounded very confusing to him. As he understood it, the hospital was in charge of transition for animals as well as humans. They were bringing in prosthetics for the animals and had opened up another surgery down there. They did a lot of rescue work for some of the local shelters. He was sure that was a never-ending job.

It would be nice to see the animals, though. He'd always loved dogs. Never been much of a cat person, but he hadn't been around them enough to find out if that was something that could change. He knew he had done more than enough today, but he was hoping maybe he could do something about that this weekend. Maybe go down and visit. The doctors told him the animals were always in need of love and care, and anytime he wanted, he could go down and comfort the ones currently in residence.

He could see horses in the fields and beautiful green rolling hills. The countryside was stunning. He'd heard bits and pieces of the history of the place, and he knew there'd been a brochure when he moved in. Something about it originally having been a veterinarian school that the Major and his daughter had transformed. That in itself was a small miracle. That they kept the animals was just kind of an odd but wonderful touch.

At first, he'd wondered if it was even sanitary to have injured people and injured animals together in the same building, then he realized they were both animals and they both needed the same kind of clean and caring environment to heal. As a plus, both could benefit from being around the other.

He really wanted to see the animals. But it was going to be a bit much today. The weekend was possible, if he made it a goal. He considered the possibility and decided it was doable.

"What's very doable?" his doctor asked, standing beside

him, a fresh cup of coffee in his hands. With a smile, Brock motioned to the chair opposite.

"I didn't realize I'd spoken aloud," he said quietly. "I'm trying to set goals for while I'm here."

"Goals are an excellent idea," the doctor said, pulling a chair back and sitting down.

"I was looking for three to achieve in the next week." Brock's ideas weren't big. In fact, they were very small. But they were something.

The doctor leaned forward. "Interesting. Tell me what they are."

"They aren't major," Brock warned. "The first is to just make it to the dining room for three meals in one day on my own." Considering how tired he was now, he didn't think he would make it back today for dinner. In fact, getting back to his room was already starting to look like a daunting prospect, but he was glad he'd tried. Now he had a better idea of what he could do when he put his mind to it. He'd need days before he tried it again.

"The second goal isn't much either," he said. "I just want to put in as much effort as I did today again."

"So today was a good day?" the doctor asked. "And putting in consistent effort is key to progress."

Brock nodded. "A hard day but one I feel good about." He knew from experience, that a great effort on one day was almost impossible to repeat on the second day. Even though he went in with the right attitude mentally, it just wasn't possible. His body needed a break afterward, and it needed to slowly build up to that level of achievement again.

"And the third?"

"The third goal was to make it down to the animal hospital every day." He smiled. "To find a dog or two to pat or even a horse. Maybe even a cat. Something with fur. Something that could use a bit of love and gives back unconditionally."

As he considered the three goals, he added a fourth. This one was harder, but it was something he needed to do. *Be more social. He needed to get out and visit with the other men. There were also a few women here, but the gender divide landed close to ninety percent on the men.*

He just needed to get out of his shell and return to life. He'd spent a lot of time locked away inside his own walls, holding the entire world responsible for his issues. Or maybe holding himself responsible for the issues and then not feeling like he could reach out to others. As if everyone would know about his guilt and therefore not reach back.

He didn't know—and he was too damned tired to work his way through it right now. The bottom line was that either way it didn't matter. Change had to happen. He had done nothing but hide since the accident, and it was time for that to stop.

Chapter 4

IT WAS ODD being at Hathaway House again. Sidney had done this back-and-forth dance between working and school for a few years now. Normally, she adjusted fairly quickly, but the last school session had been a bit rougher, thanks to John. Now, being back here again, she felt freer—more alive. It was a sobering thought how much a relationship could pull her down—make her less than she had been.

Dani had been to hell and back with her relationship before this Aaron guy showed up. Sidney was a little worried about that, to be truthful. But she hadn't been here for any of the courtship, so she wasn't sure how the guy had come across. It was always a danger to fall in love with a patient. Sometimes their situations were just so tear-jerking your heart literally went out to them. That wasn't good for them, or for you. She had always been very wary of something like that. She knew several others that had managed to pull it off and have relationships that lasted many decades afterward, and all the more power to them. But personally, she wasn't sure she could separate her professional life from her personal life in that instance.

It was almost dinnertime when she walked downstairs to see Stan. She'd hoped he was still there. He was a mainstay of the center, too. She pushed open the double doors of the veterinary clinic to still see several patients of all furry natures in the waiting room. He must have had a hell of a day if he was this backed up. As she walked across the reception area the assistant looked up and frowned at her. The name tag said Rebecca.

"Hi. Is there something we can do for you?"

Rebecca's voice was full of dread. Sidney smiled reassuringly and said, "Nope. I'm one of the therapists from upstairs. I just came down to see how you guys were doing. Actually, I've been away for nine months, and I wanted to say hi to Stan."

"Oh." Relief washed over the young woman's face. "It's been a heck of a day. He's having quite the time." She motioned with her head toward the full waiting room. "He's behind at the moment."

Just then the door opened, and Stan walked out, talking with a woman holding a small dog. As the woman left, Stan looked at the waiting room and shook his head. He turned, his gaze landing on Sidney. His face lit up, and he opened his arms. She gave him a big hug.

Sidney stepped back and said, "As much as I'd love to sit and chat, apparently you're really bogged down. Do you want me to give you a hand?"

"You so can. My assistant had to leave early today, so we're running behind."

She didn't know the ins and outs of the veterinary world, but she'd helped Stan before in the past. Between the two of them, they managed to get through the full waiting room in the next hour. When they were done, Stan slung an arm across her shoulder and hugged her close.

"Talk about good timing. I was afraid we'd never get through this day."

He walked over to one of the waiting-room couches and

sat down. Sidney studied his face, hating the fatigue in his expression. She didn't know how old Stan was but thought he appeared to have aged ten years while she'd been gone. "Sounds like you've had a rough year."

He laughed. "Rough day, yes. A rough year? No, it's been pretty decent." He looked around the room and said, "All the animal patients and their owners are gone at least, but I still have several animals that are staying overnight I have to attend to. Can you spare another half hour, then maybe we could go have dinner together?"

"I'd like that," she said with a smile. "Come on, let's get the work done first."

The first patient was a rabbit with a bad slice to its ear, which he'd had to stitch closed. While she watched, he took off the old covering on the wound and re-bandaged it. The rabbit didn't appreciate the attention it was getting, so it was Sidney's job to help keep it quiet. He was obviously a well-cared-for and beloved bunny, and quite a character. Next was a tomcat that'd had his mind changed and wasn't appreciating his new status.

"Do you actually keep these here overnight?" she asked.

"This one's a rescue. They were supposed to pick him up but asked if I could keep him overnight because they didn't have a volunteer to do the drive."

She nodded. "Makes sense."

By the time they got to the little filly outside in the fenced yard, she was immersed in the joy of being surrounded by animals. The filly walked right up to Stan and nudged him with her hand. He laughed and pulled out chunks of carrot from his pockets. He fed her a couple of smaller ones and then walked over to the older mare standing a little farther back. While Stan fed Maggie the older mare the rest of the carrots, he quickly checked over the little filly. He explained what the problem had been to Sidney. "It's a case of when people don't understand the difference between house pets and farm animals."

"I can certainly see the attraction to keeping this little one close," Sidney admitted. But it was obviously short-term thinking. She reached up and stroked the mare's long forehead. "There are more horses now, too. As usual, Dani's been busy."

"Not only are there a couple of new horses, we also have a couple of new dogs and a goat," Stan said. "I just worry she's biting off more than she can chew."

"Then it's our job to make sure she doesn't. And to help support her and this place in any way we can."

Stan laughed. "It's good to have you back, kiddo."

"Good enough that you'll feed me, now?" she asked in a teasing voice.

He reached out an elbow and she hooked her arm through his. "Shall we adjourn upstairs?" he asked with mock courtesy.

She chuckled. "Why don't we have dinner on the deck?"

They walked around the center to the back where the pool was and climbed the large stairs on that side of the center. Once again, she marveled at how much Dani had managed to do here. Not only did they have top-of-the-line equipment, but that pool really made a huge difference to the care and treatment the patients received.

The kitchen was a busy place, and the dining room was also full. At least the worst of the lineup had finished by the time they were in line. There was a large buffet, but there was always someone on the other side of the counter to help serve if needed. She chose a platter of roast beef and vegetables. She waited until Stan had pulled out a selection almost twice as large as hers, and then they carried it over to the end of the patio, down to the pool level. They listened to people splashing happily in the water, as it was open and free for everybody once therapy had finished at four o'clock. She glanced over at Stan's full plate.

"How come you never get fat?"

He chuckled. "I work too hard."

"So not nice. If I ease up on my own workouts, then all this food will go straight to my hips."

"You could use a few pounds," he said comfortably. "Besides, you're gorgeous—I wouldn't worry about it."

She wasn't sure if he was joking or not, but inside, it was nice to hear.

"Rumor says you and your boyfriend broke up already."

"Rumors." She shook her head. "I forgot what the grapevine was like here."

"Actually, I think I heard about it at the time it happened, nine months ago," he said with a wry laugh. "Sorry to hear about it, though. Any pain like that is hard to get through."

"Especially when I had such high hopes he was the one." She bent her head and focused on her full plate.

After a few minutes he said, "How's Brock doing?"

She lifted her head and looked at him silently for a few seconds. "Have you met him?"

He shook his head. "I know he's got some bigger issues than some of the guys here, but he hasn't been down to see the animals. I was kind of thinking I might be able to take Helga upstairs and pop in to say hi, but I haven't had time yet."

She sat back and stared at him. "Who is she?"

He grinned. "You can thank Aaron for that. He's been instrumental in house-training a few of the rescues—like Helga. I tell you, that dog. We're constantly building her new legs. But since Dani sprang for a 3-D printer for the center, it's actually been a lot easier than we thought it would be. Helga is a Newfoundland cross, and a huge hit with the patients. Aaron's been the one taking her around as much as he can to meet everybody."

"I don't think I've met Helga," she said.

"There's just something very appealing about her," Stan said. "Of course, there's always Chickie."

"Is Chickie still here? When I left, his owners hadn't come by to pick him up, but they said they'd be in the next day."

"They never did show up." Stan's voice was deliberately neutral.

She understood the pain. He did a lot of work for injured animals, and when the families just gave up on the animals, he was hard-pressed to find new homes for them. Sometimes it just broke his heart because the animals went into such distress and depression after they were deserted by those who had once loved them.

"Chickie is so tiny, he's perfect for carrying around to the patients as well."

"I remember him."

Stan smiled. Then he looked behind her and raised an eyebrow in question. "Hello. We haven't met." He stood and reached out a hand.

She didn't need to turn around to know who was behind her. She watched quietly as Stan and Brock exchanged handshakes. Nice and crisp—maybe a bit of measuring. There was nothing between her and Stan. They had never been anything other than kindred spirits who seemed to be hooked on the center and everything that went on around inside. She motioned toward the spare chair at the table. "Join us, Brock."

"If I may?" Brock looked over at Stan.

"Sit down." Stan resumed eating, but he kept an eye on the two of them.

Sidney made the introductions. "Anytime you want to do any work or visit with the animals, it's Stan's world down here," she said with a smile. "What that really means is, he wants you to come down and help out anytime you have a moment."

"Hey, it's not that bad," Stan protested. "It was just bad today because my assistant had to leave early."

"How many animals do you have down there?" Brock asked curiously.

"A bunny, a Maine Coon, a couple of dogs, and a snake that might end up being permanent additions, and of course Molly is out in the fields with Maggie." Stan motioned toward the pair of horses.

"Do you keep other pets here, year-round?" Brock asked, his gaze going from Stan to Sidney.

"There are several that live here all year round. Dani keeps a certain number temporarily, until we can find homes, and when they can't find homes for them, she often ends up keeping them."

Brock went still. "That's got to be a full-time job, trying to find homes for the animals, particularly if they have special needs."

"Not for her. She has the time, the patience and the inclination. But there's a very large sector of society who think we should just shoot them."

Sidney lowered her gaze, studying the lines of his face. "Are you one of them?"

"Hell, no. I'd just as soon shoot people and leave the animals in control," he said. "Anybody who can help animals gets my vote."

"Well, Dani's always looking for help. So if you're bored and you want to volunteer somewhere, there's always stuff to do."

He studied her carefully. "What kind of volunteering?"

Stan laughed. "That's what got Aaron into trouble. Now, he's going to be a permanent fixture." He pushed his chair back and stood. "If you want to come downstairs and help in my section, you're always welcome to. Every one of those animals needs to be loved and cuddled the same as every human. Then, there's always the issue of cleaning cages, taking animals for walks, taking them outside to do their business, etcetera. There is never a shortage of things that need to be done around here."

Sidney watched him walk away.

"He seems to really care," Brock said.

"He's been here for a long time, and he really does care. He's helped thousands of animals that would've otherwise been put down."

"It's a very strange place here, having animals and people together." He played with the handle on his coffee cup and then raised his gaze to Sidney. "Not bad … just … unique."

Sidney nodded. "There needs to be more creative thinking when it comes to healing," she said. "I've heard of several old-folks' homes opening day care on the premises. Having little children around isn't for everyone," she said. "But for many seniors it's been a godsend. It's poured new life into their lives. As long as it's open, and people can come and go when they want to, and it's not overwhelming with the noise and the crying of younger children, it seems to work out well. These are just a few pilot projects, but I'd love to see similar ideas spread across the country. I think the same applies for animals. Just as we have therapy dogs and therapy pets we bring into old-folks' homes and day care, hospitals and hospices, there's no reason not to have them on a more permanent basis, like here. In fact, this was originally a veterinarian school. Then Dani's father, the Major, altered it. It was a slow process, but this is the end result."

"The Major?"

Sidney laughed. "If you haven't met him yet, you will know him when you see him. He makes a point of stopping in to talk to everybody. He's in his late sixties, and he has white, bushy hair and a big, white beard."

A comical look came over Brock's face. "I've met him. I just now realized who he was."

"He and his daughter Dani, who you've met, as she was the one that would've brought you in and set you up originally, worked together until he eventually turned the reins over to her. She handles all the transfers and the company side of stuff. Every time I turn around, she's expanding and bringing on more staff." Sidney laughed and shook her head. "Actually, I'm blessed to be here. I've been doing training back and forth, and updating my own skills. And thankfully, every time I'm done, there's always a job here for me."

"That says a lot about how they feel about you, then," Brock said. "I have to admit that after what I saw today, you're very talented."

"Talented?" That surprised her. She sat back and studied Brock. "What we went through today took talent?"

A small smile played at the corners of his mouth. "You got me to work today," he said. "You let me put out effort I didn't realize I even had inside anymore. That took talent."

She laughed. "That took motivation—on my side and yours." She glanced at his cup and stood. "I'll grab a second cup for you while I get one for myself, if you like."

SHE SAID IT so casually, he didn't feel like it was being done because he was incapable of going to get it on his own. Because of that, he nodded and said, "Thank you." He also didn't want to curtail the social visit. She was a fascinating woman. It seemed like it had been a hell of a long time since he'd seen anything other than that cloud over his head. Not that it was gone. And it certainly wasn't likely to ever go away completely, but for the first time, he'd left it in a corner. He was able to see little bit more of the world than when he'd locked himself in and away from it all. It was something he hadn't even been aware he was doing, but somehow he'd put up all these walls and kept the world out.

It had taken a very interesting and magnetic personality for him to even realize what he had done. He knew how wrong a relationship between a patient and therapist would be in many cases, but he also knew of several that had worked out. It was also way too early to consider anything beyond having a cup of coffee. But he had to admit that she pricked his interest, like no one else had in years. Even in the years before he had his accident. His last long-term relationship was four years ago. That hadn't ended so much as dwindled away into nothing.

As he sat, pondering the changes in his circumstances, he

couldn't say if it was the location, or the change of venue, or even Sidney herself. But there was a small kernel of hope inside. Maybe he would see his way out of this mess. It always irritated him that people who weren't depressed had the best of advice for those that were. None of it made any difference because when you were depressed you couldn't see a way forward, no matter whether you did all the stuff people seemed to think you could do or not. You couldn't just force yourself to be happy. That just made you mad and angry and more depressed.

"Here you go." A cup of coffee was placed down in front of him.

He smiled. "Thank you very much."

"No problem." She put her own coffee down, and then turned and walked over to the other side of the deck. He watched her go. There was a very large black man, missing both legs, sitting, basking in the warm glow of the afternoon sunshine. Sidney reached down and gave him a hug. The two laughed and joked for a minute before she turned and headed back toward Brock. He didn't want it to seem like he was watching what she was doing, so he turned his attention to the rolling, green hills around him.

He swore he could be anywhere from California to Kentucky from the look of the place. It was stunning—the simplicity and healing energy. Maybe that was what made the difference. Maybe just being around people who had a different attitude made a difference. People came on the clock and did whatever they had to do and they left. Just as he was reaching for the cup of coffee, Sidney stepped in front of him.

His gaze started to move up to her face but stopped halfway. In her hands, she held one of the smallest critters he'd ever seen.

"What is it?"

A tiny little bark came out of it in reply.

"He's a very small Chihuahua cross," Sidney said with a smile. "He's had a really rough couple of years. His bones didn't grow properly, so he doesn't walk or jump well. But being here is bit of a godsend in that sense, as he doesn't ever seem to be on the ground. Somebody is always carrying him."

She reached out her hands. "Brock, meet Chickie. Chickie, meet Brock."

Brock stared at the small dog with its massive chocolate eyes. The little dog barked, but it came out as a tiny yelp. He shook his head in wonder. Instinctively, his hands reached out, taking up the little dog and bringing it closer to his chest. "He's so small."

"He's fully grown. Chickie's four years old."

With a satisfied smile, Sidney sat back down across from Brock and picked up her coffee. "Isaac over there tends to have Chickie on a full-time basis, but Chickie really belongs to everybody. He lives here full-time. He's a special-needs dog, and Stan looks after him. The staff here have incorporated him in with the therapy animals."

He could hear the words floating across the room. He understood what she was saying, but his attention was completely fixed on the tiny animal in his arms. His heart broke and proceeded to melt all over him. He gently scratched the animal behind his ears. Chickie had no problem cuddling in against his chest. He didn't do anything but drop his head and stare up at Brock. In fact, if Brock didn't know better, he would have been sure Chickie was saying, "More please, more." He couldn't imagine an animal being this content. "He has some very un-dog-like qualities," he said. "I'm half expecting him to purr."

Sidney laughed. "You're not the first to mention that. He's got a very laid-back personality, and because he doesn't jump and bark much, and has a fairly sedentary lifestyle, he's very catlike. He's quite content to curl up on your shoulder or sit in your lap—he does like it to be warm. One of his health issues is his body temperature is a little harder to regulate, so he's a happy camper when he's tucked up against somebody's body."

"He's beautiful," Brock said. He was horrified to hear his voice break. Moisture burned in the corners of his eyes. Oh, dear God, he hadn't cried in a decade. He certainly wasn't about to break down over a tiny dog. The instinctive impulse to give him back to Sidney was so strong, but at the same time, he couldn't bear to be parted from the small animal that was so damned accepting.

"We do have one rule here regarding the animals," she said. "Please don't feed any of them table scraps. With so many of you, the minute that becomes a thing, it's almost impossible to stop the animals—particularly the dogs—from eating everything in sight. In Chickie's case, his system is very delicate."

Brock raised his gaze and studied the number of people in the kitchen area. "Not to mention every one of them would have a weight issue within seconds at this place." He gently stroked a hand down Chickie's back. "It's a habit for most humans to share with their pets."

"Which is why I'm very specifically telling you we can't. The last time somebody fed Chickie a piece of meat off their plate, he ended up with a bowel blockage. That's not fun for anybody."

Just when he thought he should hand Chickie back, the little dog dropped from a sitting position, and curled up in his lap. That just broke his heart a little more as Chickie tucked his head to the side and went to sleep.

Chapter 5

EVEN THE NEXT morning Sidney was holding that picture close as she headed into her office—Brock cuddling Chickie. Chickie had been the happiest dog ever, and who could blame him? He was protected and loved—the two basic needs for any living thing. It was nice to see Brock in another light, as a big softie. But she knew he hadn't been brought to this place because he was a great patient. They had replaced his therapist four times already because he hadn't been a motivated man. That he'd worked for her yesterday was not something she was prepared to count on happening again tomorrow, or the day after. People often gave their all, and then backed off. Some things were just too hard to deal with on a regular basis. It was her job to keep him going.

Maybe she should bring Chickie into the sessions.

She smiled at that. Several times they had been tempted to bring animals up from downstairs. To show these men and women just how an animal was forced to deal with many of the same problems without all the support systems people had. Animals adapted much better than humans.

She snagged another cup of coffee on her way back to her desk, even though she didn't really need it. It was probably the fourth cup today, already. That was something she should look at trying to control. Too much coffee was never a good thing. She had broken the habit before, but going back to school had started her drinking it again.

As soon as she sat down, Shane walked over and placed his hands on the desk, leaning over to stare down at her. "You've been back a whole day, and I've hardly even seen you."

She leaned back and smiled up at him. Shane was one of those all-round nice guys. That didn't mean he was dull as dishwater, but for her, he was definitely not a super-exciting type of person. He was a friend, and a good one, and she had needed to cry on his shoulder more than once before. She propped her chin on her hand and said, "I haven't had time to do anything but breeze by."

He laughed. "Yep, we're pretty busy. You came back at a good time."

Sidney nodded. "So Dani said. She's already setting up interviews to bring more people on. There is a chance that Willa might come back."

Shane straightened at that. "That would be awesome if she could. I thought she was going to med school or something like that."

"I'm not sure if it was med school," Sidney said. "I do know she went back for more education but thought it was more therapy stuff."

"We probably don't need more therapists, but we could sure use some more physios."

"We never have trouble getting new people. This is an awesome place to work."

Shane walked back over to his desk and sat down, propping his feet up on the corner of the wooden surface. "You've been here for years now. It's been five years for me, almost six I think."

"Only six years," she joked. "I arrived just before you. I can see you being here for decades."

At that moment, two more physiotherapists walked in. The conversation turned to the general care of individual patients. As she participated in the conversation, Sidney was interested to hear nobody brought up the subject of Brock. Was he that difficult that nobody wanted to talk about him? Or was it because she was now handling his case, and they were waiting for her to bring him up? She didn't have a lot to say yet. Not until things got into more of a routine. Then maybe there'd be something to talk about.

She checked her watch and realized it was time to start moving. She stood and grabbed a manila folder off the desk. "Back to work for me."

As she walked out the door, Shane called behind her, "Don't forget, paperwork counts as work, too!"

She waved back with a smile. "Yeah, but that's the kind I don't like doing."

With the file in her hand, she headed down the hallway toward the large exercise room. She walked in and noted it was empty, which meant Andrew, her next patient, was running a little behind. She walked over to the large floor mats and double-checked everything was arranged and clean. She brought out two large exercise balls. Andrew had done phenomenally well since he'd arrived. He been here four months already and was looking forward to leaving in the next couple of weeks. She was fine-tuning his core muscles— even more important in his case, as he was actually missing both legs. But unlike a lot of patients, his attitude had always been excellent. Then again, he had a loving, supportive family who adored him—a wife and kids. He had a lot to live for. They all wanted him home in whatever shape he came in. It was his choice to go home as best as he could.

"There you are," a deep voice rumbled. "I'm Andrew."

Sidney turned to see Andrew walking in. He had running blades on the bottoms of his legs.

"Nice to meet you, Andrew. I'm Sidney." She grinned. "Look at you go. Aren't you the pro?"

"I've been wearing these for weeks. You just haven't been here. You were off lazing about in school, instead of being here where the real work was being done."

She laughed. "I know I wasn't the one working with you before, but I can see your progress from your file. You've done some awesome work."

He sat down on the ball as she watched, seeing confirmation in his gait she'd hoped to see. "What are we doing today?"

"Lots, but first take off both your prosthetic limbs."

He stared down at his metal legs. "There's just something really unnerving about not having them on now."

She nodded. "That's because they have become a crutch. Good ones, but a crutch nonetheless. They're great tools, but we tend to forget you have a lot of work to do without them." She opened his file. "I see you've done a lot of work on the upper body, and that's awesome. Obviously, you've done a lot of work on your thighs, and that's great, too. What I really need to see and test is how you are doing without them."

He looked at her and grimaced. "It's not very comfortable to work without them, anymore. I can, but it's much nicer with. They've become an extension of me."

"Exactly, that's the point," she said quietly. "We just have to make sure the base is as strong as can be, so if you don't have them you are just as strong."

He groaned, but he reached down and unclipped both of his prosthetics and dropped them to the side.

She walked over and picked them up carefully, and then laid them on the empty desk they had there for occasional use. She started him off doing simple core exercises on the ball while she watched. As she suspected, he'd been very good at hiding the weaknesses. His shoulders moved well, his arms and upper body strength were great, but every time he tried to do crossovers, or anything involving the lower back, there was an ever-so-slight pull, or he winced when he had to bring his other, stronger, muscles into play. That was what she needed to see. Because the body compensated, she needed to get the weaker muscles to step up and do their job. Most patients tried to avoid pain. They became very adept at making it look like everything was just perfect for the therapists. She had the benefit of fresh eyes. She could see where he was getting away with not doing the full job he needed to do.

That was too damned bad because he was going to hurt soon. But by the time he walked out of here in a couple of weeks, he would know what she meant. In the meantime, she sighed. She wondered how many times he was going to ask to go to the other therapists. They worked in teams here but sometimes a patient had a preference and the center tried to accommodate as much as possible.

She found out soon enough because his first request came at the end of that day. Daunted and tired, she walked out onto the deck and slammed down the stairs. Her day was done, dinner was ready, but she was too damned tired to even go over there. She could hear splashing in the pool below and thought maybe a swim would help.

"Hard day?" Dani asked with a light laugh. She sat down

in the chair beside Sidney and held out a cup of coffee. "Here."

"I think this is like my sixth cup today," Sidney said, accepting the drink from her friend. "I need to find something else to drink."

"There are lots of non-alcoholic options to choose from."

Sidney laughed. "I know there are. I'll find something." She glanced at Dani and her concerned expression. "What's up?"

Dani frowned slightly. "You had a session with Andrew today, didn't you?"

Sidney closed her eyes and then let out a half laugh. "I was working with him. I wondered how long it'd be before he asked for a change of therapists."

"Well, he's asked. What's the problem with him?"

"He's very good at hiding his weak spots," Sidney explained. "He's worked the most with Marsha, and I guess she didn't notice, but there's a whole muscle group that needs to be worked and strengthened. Otherwise, when the big muscles fatigue there will be nothing to hold him up structurally. Because of the lack of legs, he can't count on those to be there for him when times get tough."

"Do you think you were fair with him today?"

Sidney shook her head. She needed to explain this in layman terms. Dani was incredibly knowledgeable, but some of this was more medical than anything.

"Honestly, no. I had to be hard-ass. Because everyone had done such a great job on what they focused on that he looks great. Of course, it's easier to work the big muscles. Motivation-wise, he obviously wants to work the muscles that look good. Nobody wants to work on the muscles that hurt, and only some work has been done. The other team members have done a good job—to a point. The weaker muscles on the inside, the core, that need work, are for stability. He's done such a hell of a job that everybody looks at him with admiration now. His ego is pumped. He believes his muscles are fine, but they aren't. Not even close."

"He's planning on leaving in two weeks." Dani studied her carefully. "Are you saying he's not ready?"

"No. He's not ready. But if it matters that much to him, I could get him closer to being ready." She shrugged. "He can continue the same work at home, easily enough."

"Is this something anybody else could do?"

Sidney knew what she was asking. There was no way they worked together—with this many patients—without understanding that every therapist had a strength and every patient had a weakness.

"Absolutely. But they have to see what I've just seen and not take offense at not having seen it themselves earlier."

"Do you want me to talk to Andrew?"

Sidney shook her head. "No, it's my job. I'll do it. I'll talk to him today, and he can make a decision tomorrow."

Dani reached across and clasped Sidney's hand, giving it a light squeeze. "I'm so happy to have you home."

Dani rose and left Sidney there, sipping her coffee. That was the thing about Dani. She called it as she saw it, and in a nice way. That type of management skill was a gift. Sidney had been here off and on for years, but every time she came home the place became embedded more deeply in her heart. But even at home there was strife. One had to make compromises.

She stood, coffee in hand, and walked back to Andrew's room. She knocked on his door, pushed it open and walked in. He was sitting on his bed with his laptop. As soon as he saw her, his face shut down. She leaned against the doorway and smiled.

"When I was working with you today, I wondered how long it would take you to ask for a new therapist."

She caught the look of surprise on his face.

"Is that why you were so hard, then? You didn't want to work with me?" There was no ego involved in that question, she was happy to see. It was curiosity.

"No, not at all. But you have to understand that when you do really well, it's much easier to focus on the parts you're doing really well at. Everyone likes success. You want to make the bigger muscles stronger, but because of your accident and internal injuries and the lack of legs ... that's not enough.

"Stability is a massive factor for you. That means your core muscles, and not just that muscle group, of course. You've done some work—enough that the package is working well," she said. "But your body fat percentage is very low, so your muscles are shiny and bright, and you look model-perfect. If that's what you want, great. But I'm not concerned about the looks of the big, bad-ass muscles you're sporting because they aren't doing just fine."

She took a step inside. "I'm concerned about the days when you're really exhausted, the days you walk in and collapse on the couch because you just can't handle any more, and your back is killing you. Your stomach hurts, and your arms and shoulders hurt, and it's all because your core muscles are incapable of putting in as hard and long a day as the rest of the muscles that don't require 24/7 performance. As soon as those central muscles fatigue, every other muscle in the body has to compensate. When they have to do that, you have a cascading effect of damage. So, yes, I was hard on you. I could see what you needed to focus on. It's okay though, that you asked for a different therapist. I'm fine with that." She shrugged. "I've already spoken to Dani about it. But what you also have to decide is, do you want to leave this place the prettiest or the best you can be?"

She watched the glint in his eyes turn to anger, and she nodded. "You have overnight to make a decision. Dani has several other options ready for you. Talk to her in the morning, and she'll set you up."

"If you know exactly what I need, why didn't the others? Why didn't Marsha?"

She smiled. "Because they had become your friends and let you off easy."

With that she turned and walked out.

BROCK HAD HEARD about Sidney's afternoon with Andrew. First, it was in muted whispers then he happened to be sitting behind several of the therapists having lunch.

At first, he'd been slightly amused by her homecoming issues. Then he realized how much guts it had taken to buck the system and to step in to say and do what needed to be done. It was likely at a cost to herself. The other therapists weren't holding back in their comments, either.

"She just got back. She doesn't know what's been done or what was planned to be done. She's got no right to step on toes like that. There is such a thing as professional boundaries."

"She didn't actually do anything wrong," Shane protest-ed. "She was asked to work with a patient, she saw a problem, and with her typical focus, she dove in to solve it."

"Easy for you to say," one younger woman snapped. "He wasn't your patient."

"No, but everyone here is everyone's patient," Shane reminded her. "We're a team, and we work on many people together. If there was a problem, someone else should have caught it, too."

"Exactly, but no one did," the same woman snapped.

There was an odd silence at the table.

By now, Brock was fascinated at the inside look he was getting into a profession he'd never really acknowledged as being full of the same human trials as every other industry. Of course, there were people that did better than others in every job. There was always someone seriously gifted. It amazed him to see how different employees worked. There were always those he hated to work with and those that were fine, and then there were those that were desirable co-workers. They had a gift to see things from a completely different perspective that allowed him to open up his way of seeing things. His buddies were like that. They had unique perspectives on the world that he appreciated. Very often, people liked to live behind their closed-door perspectives, but every once in a while, there was somebody that just made you want to jump through the window and see the world in a whole different light.

He knew both sides of it all. His two friends Denton and Cole had been injured in an accident recently. He hadn't heard all the details yet as his buddies didn't like to talk about it. Of course now that he was here they only had text and the phone. Cole was actually in pretty decent shape, but he was pretty closemouthed, so Brock couldn't know for sure. He'd wanted the three of them to recuperate in the same hospital, but that hadn't worked out. He was supposed to be that much farther along in his recuperation. He just wasn't sure he was.

Then again, maybe he'd had the wrong therapists until now. As he listened to the table ahead of him still wrangling over Sidney's involvement in a case she had just taken on, and then he compared that to the work she'd just pulled out of him, he realized he really was blessed.

She was one of those gifted ones, with the ability to sense something was not quite right. She wasn't going to tolerate him holding back, and that was what he needed. He needed a kick in the ass. He'd never seen himself as a slouch, or somebody who would slack off his work for somebody else to do, but there was something about Sidney that made him step up and be present. He hadn't seen that in another therapist, yet.

He wondered if he should talk to Andrew about it. Because with all this gossip, he could see several of the patients might become worried maybe they had the wrong therapist, too. The only problem was he didn't know this patient. He'd not made any attempt to get to know the others, either. He realized this island he lived on was by choice. He didn't have to be alone. There were a lot of people going through the same things here.

He'd already tuned out the physios' conversation, but just as he was about to leave, he saw Sidney walk into the room. Instantly, the conversation at the table ahead of him froze. Silence fell. Then the younger woman who had been so upset snapped, "Well, it's time for me to leave."

"Marsha, don't," one of the other women murmured.

Marsha picked up her cup and walked past Sidney, completely ignoring her. Brock happened to be watching

Sidney's face as it happened. He saw the wry smile on the beautiful woman's lips. Of course, she knew what the other woman had done. Just as she'd made him face up honestly to his reality, he suspected she wasn't somebody to shirk her own. As he watched, she walked along the food line and picked up some yogurt and a bottle of juice before heading out to the sun. She made no attempt to join the others. She probably knew the reception would be less than warm. Brock contemplated going out to sit with her but realized this really wasn't his place, either.

He suspected there was a lot going on behind her beautiful blue eyes. Still, she looked so alone. As he slowly got to his feet, Shane, the big physiotherapist from the other table stood, ignoring the others, and strode across the room to sit across from Sidney. Sidney's face lit up and she smiled.

Brock was too far away to hear the conversation, but it was animated. Good for Shane. He glanced down at his hands and the crutch he still carried for safekeeping and slowly made his way back to his room. Shane was a big, strong, healthy male. Maybe there was something between the two of them. Lord knew, he didn't feel like he had much to offer. Seeing the two of them left him with a bittersweet taste in his mouth.

He really liked Sidney. He admired her. He had clearly seen it from the conversation around him and had already realized there was a lot to be said for her strong character. Because he knew if he had somebody that enabled him all day long, he would probably give the same poor performance himself. That wasn't what he wanted. This team needed to push him. Same as he would want a partner to push him. To support him but not to sit there cosseting him so he could step back and not face reality. As he neared his room, his phone rang. He stopped, leaned against the wall and pulled it out of his pocket. "Hey, Cole."

"Are you at Hathaway House?" Cole asked. "If you are, how is it? I've been offered a place there."

"What?" Brock asked, astonished. "That's awesome. It would be fantastic if you came."

"Really, buddy? Are you sure? You wouldn't lead me down the wrong path, right? It wouldn't be just the two of us against the place, would it?" Cole's voice held humor, but at the same time, there was a note of anxiety.

Brock laughed. "No, man. This place is different. Nothing like I've seen before. Goes to show you how different the military is from the private sector. You'll see the minute you arrive."

"Well, that's good to know. Because I sure as hell didn't want to go from this institutionalized living to something worse. I understand Denton has already applied to come to Hathaway, too, but I don't think he has coverage."

"Having the three of us together, well, that would be awesome. But you're right, I didn't even know I had all the coverage for this. I'm not sure how I got in at all, actually. I applied, but I was totally surprised when I was accepted."

"Are you sure this is a cool place to be?"

"Do you like animals?"

"You know I do, especially dogs."

"Well, they're all over this place. There's a veterinary clinic on the lower level. So, there are therapy animals in the building, and patients upstairs get to spend time with all the animals downstairs."

There was shocked silence on the other end of the line. "Damn," Cole murmured.

"You have to come and see for yourself."

"I will. And it could be earlier than you think."

On that mysterious note, Cole hung up. Brock chuckled. Life would be so different if Cole were here. He didn't
know what was happening with Denton, but damn! With a
lighter heart, and hope spreading through him, he made his
way back to his room, feeling truly happy for the first time in
a long while.

Chapter 6

"IT'S ALREADY ALL over the place," Sidney said in a low voice.

"Of course, it is. Like any workplace, rumors and gossip happen sometimes."

Sidney nodded and scooped up a bite of her yogurt. "Yeah, I probably wasn't the most subtle person on the planet. Came out like an elephant in a china shop."

Shane gave a big belly laugh that had several other patients looking over at him.

She shook her head. "It's not that funny."

"Oh yes, it is. It's not that you're an elephant in a china shop, but you call it as you see it in that direct, forthright way that is not terribly welcomed by everybody."

She nodded. "I stepped on people, and hurt their feelings, right?" Damn, she hated doing that.

"I'm not so sure if it's you, or if it's professional courtesy—or lack thereof."

She leaned back. "Well, there are a lot of things I'd apologize for, but that's not one of them."

"Do you really see a problem with Andrew?" Shane asked curiously. "I never worked with him myself."

She studied him and said, "If you have a slot open, maybe you should. He'd probably get along well with you. He should not be around young pretty women."

Shane's eyebrows rose. "What, am I a mean old ugly troll?"

"No, but you're not likely to be susceptible to his charms."

Understanding slammed into his eyes. "Then maybe I should ask to take him on. He's only here for another couple of weeks."

She nodded, feeling better. "That would actually be a very good thing." She sighed. "Do I have to apologize to Marsha?"

"Honestly, I'd leave it. You don't think she did the best job she could. I'll find out myself tomorrow morning, but at this point, if you bring it up with anyone it will make it worse."

"As long as I'm not taking on any other people she's been working with," Sidney said. "That's not likely to work out so well."

"That's another thing I'm wondering. I'm not sure, but I think he managed to request her for the entire duration, which is not a good thing. I know they became great friends, but that's not always the best situation."

Sidney frowned. "That shouldn't have happened. Every therapist has their strengths and weaknesses."

"We have teams for each patient," he reminded her. "But members do shifts. The therapists always rotate through." He frowned as he looked across the table at the group of therapists he'd left. "At least, normally, we shift them around. If not, then we need to have a talk with Dani about doing more of that. I think it's been kind of loose up till now."

Sidney was silent for a moment. "I think you're right. I think we do need to switch around." Then she laughed. "But

I rocked the boat enough for one day."

She finished her yogurt and coffee and stood. "Thanks for coming over, Shane."

He was sprawled lazily in his chair, his long legs stretched out along the deck. "Not a problem."

She brought her dirty dishes to the shelf in the kitchen, and then made her way back to her room. Her quarters were on the far side of the building, and on the lower level. Several staff members lived on the premises, and a number didn't. It was a personal choice, and, of course, it also depended on space. She'd given up her small apartment when she went back to school, but it'd been recently vacated, so she was back in her same digs. She walked into the studio and collapsed on the bed. She rubbed her face with her hands. She really had to handle things better. That was her fault. She should've considered the previous therapist and not been quite so adamant. But like everything else, it was over, and there was only so much she could do now.

What she could do, however, was go for a swim. She got up and changed into her suit and cover-up, grabbed a towel and made her way to the pool. There were a lot of advantages to living on the premises—not only the meals but also the exercise facilities. After the day she'd had, her own muscles needed a bit of a workout. She'd love a massage, too, but that wasn't likely to happen. Often, the therapists worked on each other on an exchange basis. However, she figured she was probably out of the loop right now, and not likely to get back into it anytime soon.

There were several people on the pool level when she got there. She ignored them all and dropped the towel and cover-up on one of the chairs in the sun, walked to the end and dove into the water at the first lane.

As soon as the cold water closed over her head, a sense of peace and serenity filled her body and soul. She broke the surface to gasp for air, and then struck out strongly for the other side, once again filled with that sense of rightness. She'd never been one to not rock the boat if the boat needed to be rocked. Hopefully, now that she'd caused whatever turmoil was rolling on around her, things would work out and ease back down again.

There was always an adjustment to getting back to work, the same as it was going back to school.

She just wanted this adjustment to pass by quickly because she'd like to settle down and get to work again. That's where she excelled.

Although, apparently, she didn't excel quite so much in her professional and patient relationships. Suddenly, she felt slightly overwhelmed, wondering why she'd ever bothered coming back. She swam faster.

She really hoped tomorrow was going to be better.

BROCK SETTLED INTO his room, feeling a sense of peace and quiet. Now that he knew his friends could possibly be coming here to be with him, he felt energized. In need of something to do, he grabbed his crutches and left his room. He knew that his body had taken a hell of a workout today, and he didn't want to trust losing his balance and falling.

He hobbled over to the elevator and headed down to the vet clinic. He smiled at Stan, who was talking with a couple of patients holding cats in cages. He grinned and headed to Rebecca, the receptionist.

"Stan said he wouldn't mind having a few volunteers. I

don't have a ton of energy, but maybe there is something small I can do to help out."

The middle-aged woman looked up at him and smiled with a wide happy-go-lucky grin on her face. He immediately fell under her trance.

"A little bit of energy for hugs?" she asked. "Or a little bit more energy for cleaning cages? Depending on how ambulatory you are, we have a couple of dogs that need to go outside to do their business ..."

He glanced down at the crutches and said, "I probably could take the dogs out to do their business as long as they don't knock me down."

She stood and glanced at the crutches. "Two of them are recovering from surgery and should be going home in a couple of days, so they're not exactly jumping around and hyper. I'll bring you one and see how you do."

He waited for a few minutes while Stan said goodbye to the two women, and then turned and walked over to say hi to him.

"Hi, Brock, it's nice to see you down here." He motioned at the crutches, "How are you doing today?"

"I'm doing just fine. I had a hell of a workout today, so I'm feeling the effects, but I was still a little too keyed up to spend the rest the night in my room."

"Who's your therapist?"

"Sidney." Brock watched as Stan's face lit up. "She took more out of me and made me pull more out of myself than I've ever had any therapist do. I gather she's going through a bit of a tough patch right now, but I've never had a therapist like her."

Stan's face cleared. "I'm really glad to hear that. She's a hell of a girl. She really cares about her patients, but she'd be the first to say she's less concerned about her relationships with everybody than she is about fixing what's wrong with the body."

"You know, I'm okay with that," Brock said. "I've listened to enough platitudes and empty promises, so when I find somebody who actually means what they say and does what they say, well …"

Just then, Rebecca came back with a Basset hound walking at her side.

"Oh, I think I can handle this guy." He was kind of relieved because he didn't want a dog that would trip him up, or a big one that might decide to drag him down the yard. He had been half afraid he was taking on more than he could handle.

"This is Marshall. He had a cyst removed, so he isn't moving superfast. But he has the same need to go outside as everybody." She turned to look over at Stan and said, "Do you want to grab Major and take him at the same time? That was the last patient for the day so …"

"Sure, I can do that." Stan started to walk in the opposite direction, but he turned and called back, "Just give me a minute."

Considering Brock had no idea where he was going, that was probably a damned good idea. He idly glanced around at the clinic and realized just how open and friendly it all looked. He turned back to Rebecca.

"How long have you worked here?"

"Years and years and years," she said with a laugh. "And I hope to be here years and years more."

"That's a hell of a good reference for coming here," Brock said. "It seems to be a thriving business."

She nodded. "It is, but we do a lot of charity work too."

Stan walked out leading a very large Great Dane. It was a little sprightlier than the Basset hound but not much. Brock let the Great Dane and Stan go ahead, and then he followed behind. The Basset walked slowly at his side. He realized he needn't have worried. In this case, it was the injured leading the injured. He was glad to be able to do it. Outside, there was a large dog run. Stan walked to the gate, opened it and held it open while Brock walked in.

"Just unclip the dogs and let them wander. There are only the two of them today."

It took a little bit of coordination, but Brock finally managed to unclip the leash from the Basset hound. He hobbled to the side of the pen, watching the two dogs carefully explore. They truly seemed to enjoy being in the fresh air. He agreed—he felt the same way. He glanced around to see several horses in one paddock, and beside them were a little, tiny foal and an older mare. Someone was talking with them. As he watched, Sidney threw her arms around the little baby and hugged her. Then she let it go, to watch the little horse dance and prance around her. Her laughter floated on the wind. He smiled.

That was what she needed. She couldn't have had an easy day. She turned and caught sight of them and waved. He waved back. He turned to see Stan grinning like a fool.

"She's quite something, isn't she?" Brock asked. In his heart, he was hoping there was no relationship between the two of them. There'd be at least more than a decade of age difference, but he'd seen many that had a lot more. Still, he couldn't imagine anybody telling Sidney that was a no-no because of some nefarious rule she didn't believe in. He knew she'd go where she wanted to regardless.

Stan nodded. "She's a really great lady."

Frowning Brock turned back and watched her reach over and hug the mare. "She seems to be comfortable with the animals."

"She comes down here a lot. She spends all day helping people up there, but who's to help her when she runs into trouble?" Stan's voice was sad.

"You know her well, don't you?"

"There are not too many up there I don't know. But for those who have been here as long as I have," he corrected himself, "we're family."

Brock knew he shouldn't say anything but was unable to help himself. "Is there anything more than that there?"

Stan shot him a look, and then he laughed. "No, not at all. She's like a little sister to me. They all are. For all the relationships that have come and gone, I've never met anybody here for me, unfortunately." He shrugged his shoulders and gazed straight back over to Sidney. "Her last relationship broke up on the first day of going back to school. It was pretty rough timing."

"That would be," he said sympathetically. Inside, Brock was elated. If she didn't have a partner, then that meant the field was open. He didn't even know how she felt about him. He sure as hell hadn't given her a great impression at the beginning, but he was starting to understand she wasn't going to be all that easy to care for, either. But sometimes one had to work for the best things in life.

He had a few months here. Maybe they could make some progress. At least he hoped so because he realized he'd been thinking about her all day long. As she walked over to the two of them, he brightened.

She stopped on the other side of the fence and crossed her arms on the top rail. "I'm surprised to see you here,

Brock. I'll have to work you harder next time," she teased.

But the smile didn't reach her eyes. Instead, he could see the deeper concern. He finally realized what Stan had been talking about. He was right. She looked after her patients all day long, but when she had a low spot, who was there for her? Taking a chance he said, "I'm enjoying gaining comfort from the animal world."

She raised one eyebrow and nodded. "So ..." She looked down at the Basset and smiled. "Who is this guy and what happened that he's here?"

The three of them looked at the Basset as Stan went over Marshall's medical history. "He's come a long way."

The Great Dane wandered around and didn't appear to be interested in doing anything other than enjoying the fresh air and being with people. That, and he was probably in a cage for most of his time here, which wasn't nice for anybody.

"Do these animals have homes?"

"Both do," Stan replied. "They have families that love them. But so often we are the home for those that don't."

"Right, the charity work here the receptionist mentioned."

"I do a lot of that. But we couldn't manage to do it all without Dani. She somehow gets us funding when we run short. She has a charity set up and receives donations through that. Luckily, she seems to know a lot of money-people willing to donate, and that keeps the place moving, both upstairs and downstairs."

Chapter 7

S HE WAS GLAD to see Brock here, although she shouldn't be. The animals were a hell of a tug on the heartstrings. He'd been tired out, but now he looked … content. So, something had changed in his world. She wished something had changed in hers. She knew tomorrow was a whole new day, and she wished it was tomorrow already.

"You've been swimming?" Stan asked.

She felt Brock's glance as she nodded. "Even then, I was still too keyed up, so I decided to come out and walk around to reacquaint myself with all my old friends." The old mare had followed her over and nuzzled her hand. She laughed and stroked the long velvet nose. "This is Maggie."

Twisting, she wrapped her arms around Maggie's neck. "She's been here as long as I have—much longer, in fact."

"And shall be here for a lot longer still," Stan said with a smile. "She's in great health."

Sidney turned and headed back toward the gate. "I'm going to head back to my place. I'll see you two tomorrow." She watched as a flash of something that looked like disappointment crossed Brock's face.

Impulsively, she said, "Unless either of you want to join me for a coffee?"

Stan shook his head. "I'm not done for the day yet." He turned to Brock and said, "You go on. I'll take both dogs back in."

"Are you sure?"

"Yes, you go ahead."

Sidney laughed like a little kid as Brock tried to hobble quickly behind her.

Somehow, she knew this was going to be fun.

And it was. Like two kids, they enjoyed a cup of coffee and conversation. No pressure. No strings. Nothing but two people who enjoyed spending a quiet hour together. She didn't keep him long. She was tired, too. And by the time she headed to her room, she was smiling.

The next day dawned bright and cheerful with a blue sky and sunshine. She'd gone to bed in a much happier frame of mind. As far she was concerned, yesterday was done and over with. With any luck, she could just move forward and get into a normal routine of being here. She checked her watch and realized she didn't have enough time for another swim. That was something she was going to have to adjust her schedule for. Fitness was important, particularly with all the food readily available.

She dressed quickly, walked upstairs and grabbed a coffee, then stepped out onto the deck. Standing at the railing, she studied the rolling hills and the animals. They really could bring in twenty to forty more horses without any difficulty. The lush grass could certainly support them. It might actually be a way to bring in income for the center, too. Rent out the paddocks and pastures. There were a lot of horse people around town. The only thing was, someone would need to keep an eye on them, and that was going to require yet more staff. Therefore, it might not cover the costs. She wasn't sure how a business plan would work.

The eating area was still empty except for one or two

people. Turning back to refill her coffee, she sent up one more silent wish that today would be an upswing day. At that moment, Shane and Marsha walked in. Marsha stiffened, grabbed a coffee and turned her back on Sidney. Shane smiled at her. "Good morning."

Grateful for his friendship, she said, "Good morning back at you. It's a beautiful day today."

"It is indeed." He grabbed himself a coffee, snagged a muffin and followed Marsha.

There was no invitation to join them. Sidney shrugged. Why would there be? She supposed it didn't help that she still felt more like a guest than an employee. Walking back to the buffet, she picked up a selection of yogurt, granola, and fruit, and took it back out to the sunshine. She sat down to enjoy her food with her back to the dining area. When a shadow fell across her, Sidney stiffened apprehensively.

"Can I join you?" Brock's deep voice smoothed over her.

She beamed a smile up at him. "Sure."

"You didn't look like you wanted company, so I wasn't sure." He pulled out a chair and sat down.

"Not to worry. It's fine." Always the therapist, she studied him critically. His color was good, but she could see the heavy lines of fatigue on his face from the workout the day before. She'd already known that today would have to be an average day, not another hard-working one. "Did you have a good night?"

He nodded. "Not bad. Still woke up a bit on the tired side, though."

"Is that so?" She smiled at him crookedly and went back to eating.

"This'll blow over," he said in a low voice, pointing with his chin to the other physiotherapists inside.

"Maybe. Maybe not." She turned to study the table were Marsha and Shane were sitting. "We're all professionals here. Some of us just have different techniques, and some of us are a little more abrasive than others." She gave him a lopsided smile. "You know which of these applies to me."

"It's what makes the world go round." He smiled at her, a lopsided grin that tugged at her heart. He was a good-looking man. Now that they'd gotten over their initial dustup, she looked forward to a solid, working relationship.

She checked her watch and said with a grin, "Are you ready for me to crack the whip?"

He snorted. "Yes. But I have forty-five minutes first, and I want every damn minute." Then he laughed. "Hopefully not too much cracking."

"It won't be quite so tough today."

He raised an eyebrow at her. "Getting soft on me?"

She chuckled. "Not a hope in hell. But every muscle needs a chance to recover." She waggled her eyebrows and leaned forward. "Just think—there's lot of muscles we can still work on while those are resting."

He winced.

She went off into gales of laughter. Finally composing herself, she added, in a conspiratorial whisper, "That's okay, baby, I'll be gentle." She stood and walked away, still chuckling.

"Promise?"

Sidney froze. Then, she turned and shot him an uncertain look, grateful to find his gaze fixed on his coffee cup before she hurried out the door. Only, the thought wouldn't leave her alone.

It seemed like for the last few days and weeks, all she had seen were couples kissing or exchanging special smiles, hands brushing against cheeks, wonderful loving gestures. Just the knowledge that the two people in question were in a special relationship. The world really was built for twos. As a single, it was an odd feeling to see so many other happy couples, particularly when she didn't have anybody coupled up to her. Did she want to be? Maybe. It had been nine months since her relationship had gone to pieces. It was certainly long enough to get over it, but she also hadn't found anybody else who attracted her. Immediately, her mind drifted toward Brock. She really liked him. She could tell a lot about the character of a person when she worked with them. So far, she'd found absolutely nothing to not admire.

He was also sexy as hell. So many men felt their sexuality went out the window when they'd lost a limb, when they were so badly injured there were physical deformities. She worked with injured men and women every day, all day. To her, the beauty of a person came from the soul inside. She could sympathize with the injuries, but it was her job to help make the person as strong, fit and as capable as they could be. To do that, she connected with the inner spirit that was unique to each person. Brock instantly came to mind. She had to admit he was unique.

She smiled as a tiny tingle went down her spine. She'd love to spend more time with him. But he needed to heal and strengthen, so he could move on. And then Brock would leave. So what good would it do to start a relationship now? Unless they were going to end up in the same town down the road, the chances of them being able to have a relationship weren't very good. Plus, she wasn't into clandestine affairs with patients. Even if Dani had opened the doors to that possibility.

Sidney understood because love was like that. Now, it

also allowed her to pursue a relationship with Brock, if she wanted to. And, she realized belatedly, she wanted to. Her thoughts were constantly on this man. And she knew he was of the same mind, with the same heartstrings tied in knots as she was.

Being in a relationship where one person settled sucked. She understood the theory, the philosophy that in every relationship somebody settled, but she didn't agree with that. She thought there were lots of relationships where people came in as equals. She wanted to believe that because if it wasn't true when she went wholeheartedly into a relationship and felt one hundred percent committed, that meant the other person was settling. And that was not what she wanted. She wanted someone to look at her as being good enough without any of the other limiting factors. She wanted someone to look at her and to feel humbled to have her in their life. In the same way as she had felt humbled to have her past relationships be a part of her world. The last thing she wanted was to consider that somebody had *settled* for her.

IT WAS SEVERAL days later when Brock returned to his room after a particularly testing morning trying to sort himself out. The counselor had not been one bit of help. He also hadn't liked the news from the doctor this morning and had been trying to reach his buddy Cole all day, with no response. He sat down on his bed and stared, dispirited, out the window. For all that had happened, this was a great place to be, yet his life right now still sucked.

He had just enough time to get a shower before lunch. If he didn't get to lunch early then there was going be a huge line. He headed into the bathroom and refused to give himself a chance to just stand under the hot water as he wanted to do. Finally redressed, he was about to pocket his phone when it buzzed in his hand.

He pulled the device out to see who had texted him. Cole. He read the message. **Where the hell are you?**

He answered back. **I'm where the hell I always am. Where the hell are you?** He frowned, confused by the message. Another text popped up on his screen with a soft ping. **Maybe you should come to the dining room and see for yourself.**

His heart jumped. **What?** He bolted down the hallway as fast as he could, making his way to the dining room. As he stood in the doorway, he scanned the huge room full of people. Was he really here? Why didn't he tell him when he was coming in? They'd been friends for decades. They had been in high school together. They'd taken different paths for a while, but then both had ended up in BUD/s training together. Seeing Cole and Denton in the same training camp at the same time had been both unnerving and hugely comforting. They'd supported each other all the way through the brutal training. But they'd passed. They'd actually survived, and they knew it was partly because of the support they'd given each other.

BUD/s wasn't the kind of training one did on one's own. Not that you couldn't, but the journey was a ton easier if you had somebody to help you get there. He'd put his own success down to having his friends there. They'd ended up on different SEAL teams over the years, and they'd gone on several missions together, but not as many as he'd have liked.

His gaze landed on the beloved, scarred face in the sunshine. He hobbled as fast as he could.

By the time he reached Cole, his buddy was standing, one crutch under his arm and tears in his eyes.

They hugged.

Damn, his heart was breaking with joy.

Chapter 8

GOOD NEWS TRAVELED fast at Hathaway. Often, patients created friendships there that survived even long after the individuals had returned to their normal lives. Sidney didn't remember ever seeing two patients that had been friends beforehand coming here together, though. It would prove to be an interesting dynamic. Would they help each other or enable each other to do less? She was looking forward to finding out, particularly when one of them was Brock. She knew he'd had a hard adjustment here. A friend might be a good answer. At the same time, part of her was sad and maybe a little jealous. Her time away had isolated her somewhat from the other staff and until now, she'd enjoyed spending the time with Brock. Now he was going to want to spend his time with Cole.

Maybe that was good. A new perspective on his care and their relationship couldn't be a bad thing. She walked into his room with a bright smile pasted on her face. Already, she noticed a change. He sat on his bed, his back and shoulders straight, and a smile on his face as he texted on his phone. She had no doubt who he was talking to.

"Don't you look bright and happy this morning."

He looked up, and his grin brightened. "Absolutely," he said with a laugh. "A buddy of mine is here now, too. It's so great to see him."

She smiled. "Does that mean you can work harder and better and faster now?"

He laughed. "Well, I don't know about that. I seem to do plenty of that as it is when I'm around you." He motioned at his phone. "It's just nice to see somebody you know. Somebody who understands where you've been, and what you're up against. And know the same about them. It's not that misery loves company, but everyone needs ..." A slight grin slid out. "... maybe understanding."

"That's normal. As much as we do understand, in that we see people like you day in and day out, we are not in your position," she said lightly. "So we can empathize and commiserate, but we haven't walked in your shoes, so we can't really understand."

"Exactly," he said, nodding his head emphatically. "You actually get it. More than I expected."

"Well then, you understand it's time to get to work."

He gave her a mock salute. "Lead on, commander."

She shook her head. "It's the other way around. You lead on. We're going to start in the weight room this morning. Let's go see what you can do today."

He hopped up easily, then he strode out of the room. He didn't take a crutch for balance or safekeeping. She smiled behind his back as she walked. He was doing so well. With any luck, he'd be out of here quickly. Not that that would make him terribly happy, if his friend had just arrived. But she didn't know that for sure. He did have a lot more to do on his back, that was for certain. She set him up with some exercises to get started. Light warm-ups, then she'd start checking out some of the muscles.

"Sidney?"

She turned to see Shane in the doorway.

"Give me a minute." She turned back to see how Brock was doing.

He waved her off and said, "This is just a warm-up. I promise, I won't hurt myself."

She raised her eyebrows at the cockiness in his attitude. He certainly had a lot more energy and a lot more enthusiasm this morning, and that was a good thing. She turned back to Shane and said, "What's up?"

"Andrew is being discharged in a couple of days," he said. "I wanted you to see how he's doing."

"There's no need for me to see him," she said. "I trust you to do a good job."

Shane laughed. "Actually, I think he doesn't trust anybody else now. Not that he would admit it."

She frowned at him. "What do you mean?"

"You were right," he said simply. "A couple muscle groups hadn't been given enough attention, and they needed work. Once he realized the truth of what you had said, he got really angry. Then he buckled down to work."

"He seemed like the kind of guy that would do that." She nodded. "I'm glad you took him on."

"Now he doesn't want to listen to my take that he's doing much better. He knows he's leaving in a couple of days and is afraid there hasn't been enough progress. But it's not required, and the cost of the bill would land in his lap if he stayed longer than prescribed."

She studied his face. "And?"

Shane leaned against the doorjamb and crossed his arms as he looked toward where Brock was working. "It's actually a request from Andrew. He would like to know if you could possibly come and take a look, to see where he might still be lacking."

Sidney blinked, and then she laughed. "So the guy that sent me away, complained about me and wanted to change to yet another therapist now wants me to make sure the work's been done properly?"

"Absolutely," Shane said with a crooked smile. "As you're the one that found the problem before, he would like to know you approve of the changes and you don't see anything new that concerns you."

Amused, she grinned. "Where is he now?"

"He's in the room next door."

She turned to look back at Brock. "I don't want Brock to be alone. Give me ten minutes, and we'll move over there. That way, I can keep an eye on both of them." She gave him a wry smile. "It's going to feel weird, though."

Shane squeezed her shoulder. "You did what you needed to do, and he had to learn." He turned and left the room.

She walked back to Brock and pushed him through the rest of the set she had established.

"So, we're changing rooms?" he asked.

Of course, he'd overheard the conversation. "Do you mind?"

"Nope, as long as it doesn't change what we're working on."

She grabbed his gear and motioned for him to go ahead. By the time he reached the door, she'd given the equipment a quick wipe-down and followed him.

In the other room, she could see Shane and Andrew standing and talking.

She studied Andrew, assessing his balance and his relaxed stance. Then, when he saw her, he straightened. She noted his stiff bearing but also that he stood strong. There was no leaning to the side.

"How much work is there to be done this morning?" she asked Shane.

"About an hour."

She nodded. She studied Andrew for another long moment. She walked around him. She knew he was a little confused, but she kept a smile on her face.

Brock reached out and shook Andrew's hand. "I hear you'll be leaving soon."

Andrew shook his hand warmly in return. "There are definitely worse places to be, but there's no place like home."

Brock chuckled in agreement. He nodded at Sidney and said, "I'll head over to the balls and do some more stretching before you come over and give me the drill-sergeant routine." With a goodbye smile at Andrew, he walked over to the chairs on the other side of the room to give them a bit of privacy.

Shane laughed. "I see he knows you well."

She gave him an amused smile. "Apparently I have a bad reputation here." She turned back to Andrew and said, "If you don't mind, can I get you to walk toward the door and then turn around and walk back to me. Walk straight and as naturally as you can."

He raised one eyebrow but obediently turned and walked toward the door and then, using the doorjamb, he turned around and walked back to her.

"Did you need the doorjamb for support?" she asked. "Or was it just habit?"

He frowned at her in confusion, then he looked at the door. "I'm not sure. I guess I have to figure that out." He turned on his own just fine and walked back to the door again. He passed through the doorway back and forth several times and said, "I think it's a habit."

"But you are favoring your left leg. Did you hurt it?"

He glanced down at his leg and said, "I accidentally cut it with my fingernail last night. It was surprisingly deep and irritated me. It surprised me how sensitive it is."

"Any injury on the stumps will take longer to heal. Until you build up the eventual callus there, you'll notice every little bump and scratch," she said calmly. She glanced over at the exercise balls and back at him. "Are you up for a few exercises?"

He winced. "I guess we're back to the same ones I did originally for you?"

She nodded. "I want to see how much improvement there is."

Andrew glanced over at Shane.

"It's all good," Shane said.

Andrew walked to the balls and removed both prosthetic limbs. She led him through a series of exercises to determine what the inner abdominal muscle groups were doing. Finally, he sat back up, his breathing strong and his face flushed. "Damn, this is hard work."

"Hard work it might be, but you did fine." She walked over to Shane and held out her hand for his clipboard. "You're still favoring the left side, but you've come a long way. I knew we would be able to get you there, but without some extra work, you aren't going to be able to maintain it. Going home will throw you off. There, you will twist and turn, bend and use muscles in ways you haven't in a long time, so that's going to put strain on your system. You need to maintain physio for several months. Shane will give you a set of exercises to keep you strengthening that muscle group."

She finished writing down the notes for Shane's chart

and handed it to him. She smiled at Andrew. "Other than that, you've done a lot of work and it's paid off. You're looking good." She reached out and shook his hand. "Congratulations. I hope you have a great future."

She patted Shane on the shoulder and turned to head over to Brock.

IT WAS HARD not to hear their conversation, but Brock focused on his workout, trying to give them privacy. There'd been enough rumors going around for the past week, and he realized this was a happy conclusion for Sidney. And for Andrew, by the looks of it. He wondered how he would feel if another therapist had said there was something missing in his workout, and that his current therapist hadn't done as good a job as possible. It would be scary. In Andrew's case, he was heading back home without the support he'd had here for so many weeks, if not months. To think that at the last minute something had almost been missed … well, that was one of the worst scenarios he could imagine.

For him, he had been assigned to Sidney on her first day back, and she'd done a hell of a job with him. Still, he had to wonder—what if a different therapist did see something else? Should one have multiple therapists because they each would see something different?

He knew it was that way in many industries. What one chef knew, another one didn't always know. What one editor saw wrong in a project, another editor would see differently. It wasn't bad, it was just the way the world was. He'd had other therapists before coming here, and he hadn't done well with them. Now that he was supercharged and starting to feel like his old self again, did it mean another therapist wouldn't see something different?

He had had Shane before. Apparently, Shane and Andrew had gotten along well, if what he'd seen these last several weeks was anything to go by. In fact, Shane and Sidney seemed to get along fine, too. A little too fine for his liking.

Brock gave his head a shake. He had no business thinking like that, but he was a single, healthy male, Sidney was stunningly attractive, and it was pretty damned hard not to. He'd spent a ton of his spare time with her. He couldn't wait to talk to Cole about her. Just the thought of seeing his friend at lunchtime made him move into his workout with a ferocity he hadn't seen in himself since Sidney's first day.

"Hey, killer, what's the rush?" Sidney asked with a smile.

Brock could see she was truly happy. Something had been settled inside. She was happy with Andrew now and the outcome of the problem. He had no idea how the other therapist would react, but he hoped none of it would come back on Sidney.

"I'm meeting Cole for lunch today," he said happily, pushing away that train of thought. "I can't wait."

She smiled. Hmm. Maybe things weren't perfect, yet. She was a little subdued. He gave her a bright smile, hoping he could infuse some of his good humor into her for the day. He was feeling fantastic. The happy mood kept up all the way through the morning workouts. By the time they broke for lunch, he was feeling damned proud of himself.

He headed back to his room and had a quick shower, then made his way to the dining area. He grabbed a chair at a table out in the sunshine—his favorite—off to the left by the horses and texted Cole. **I'm at lunch and I've got a**

table for us.

And he waited.

And waited some more. Frowning, he rose and headed to the buffet. He was hungry and really didn't want to wait any longer. Besides, he had no idea what was holding his buddy up. He hadn't even texted back. So ... was there a problem? He cast his mind back to his first few days at Hathaway, and the teams he had to meet, and all of the testing that had to be done. He realized that if nothing else, Cole was likely exhausted and possibly asleep.

He could also be eating in his room.

Sobered, and remembering the harsh adjustment at the beginning of his own journey, Brock returned to the table he'd chosen out in the sun and ate his lunch alone.

Chapter 9

SIDNEY SAT ON the first table on the deck side of the dining room, watching as Brock walked in and took his place. She wondered about joining him for a moment, then remembered he was waiting for Cole. When he got his own lunch and headed back alone, she pondered for a second time if she should join him. But there was something going on between him and his friend, and she didn't want to get in the way. She was happy to support him if there was something there to be supportive of. But she'd have to wait for him to tell her about it. Shane dropped down in the chair opposite her with his tray full of food. She jumped in surprise.

"At least you're still talking to me," she said wryly.

"Of course. But then I'm a male."

She snorted. "There is definitely a difference between working with a group of females versus a group of males." As a female, she understood her own sex well. She had little tolerance for a lot of their foibles. But there were a lot of good things about women that men just couldn't compete with. Shane did a very good job of dodging bullets with all the women as it were. In fact, she wondered why he was single. He was gorgeous, compassionate, extremely professional and very good at his job.

"How come you've never hooked up with anybody

here?" she asked.

Startled, he stopped with his fork in midair, and then shook his head, popping the food into his mouth, a big grin on his face. When he finally could speak, he said, "Sidney, you need to work on your interrogation tactics."

"Why? It's a simple question." She picked up her coffee cup and studied him over the rim. "You're good looking. You're personable, and you're very professional. What's not to like?"

He gave a small shrug and said, "You tell me. There have been a couple women here I've liked, but it didn't work out."

She nodded. "That's too bad."

"I'm not too bothered. I figure I'll find somebody sometime. In the meantime I'm more than a little busy with my career."

She glanced back toward Brock, only to find he was laughing at something on his phone. "I hear you. With all the people coming and going in this place, it's a steady job just keeping up with the names."

"Speaking of people coming and going, Cole had a rough adjustment."

She looked over at him. "How rough?"

"He won't be doing therapy for a week or two. The doctors need him to regain his strength, first. The trip here took more out of him than anyone expected. And he pushed it as soon as he got here."

"Which means he hasn't fully recovered from his latest surgery. I'm sorry for Brock. He was so excited about meeting his buddy for lunch. But when he didn't show up, I see he ate alone."

"There could be many days like that."

"It happens." She made a mental note to have a talk with Brock later. Just because he was moving in leaps and bounds didn't mean his friend was going to follow. One had to be very respectful of everybody's progress. She spent a few minutes sitting with Shane while he ate, and then made her excuses. She took her cup of coffee and snagged an apple as she walked out. She had fifteen minutes before she had to go work on schedules and reports, and then she had a full afternoon. She walked to Brock's room to find the door shut. She stood in the hallway and frowned. Not wanting to see his mood affect his performance, or put his recovery in jeopardy, she decided on knocking.

"Who is it?" came the voice from inside the room.

"It's me, Sidney."

There was kind of an odd silence, then he said, "Come in."

She turned the knob and stuck her head inside. "Hey, you doing okay?"

His expression was a cross between frustration and disappointment. Something wasn't right, and she was willing to bet it was Cole.

He gave a shrug. "I'm fine."

"Well, you're not, but that doesn't mean you're ready to share." She took a step into the room and waited. "This is about Cole?"

His gaze flew up to her. "What do you know about Cole?"

"I know he's had a rough introduction, and it's going to take several days before he is likely even allowed out of bed." She was surprised at Brock's dark eyes and could see the myriad possibilities whirring away in the back of his gaze.

"I haven't seen him myself," she rushed to say. "But as

far as I know, there is nothing major. Sometimes traveling and the change can set people back for a day or two, and they just need time to adjust—time to breathe. That's what I would suspect is the issue with Cole."

"He's a good guy." He gazed down at his bed and nodded. "But he also isn't the best at following orders."

Her heart went out to Brock. He was really worried about his buddy. "I'm sure he is. Chances are, he's sound asleep and will likely sleep the bulk of the next two days to recover."

When he looked up at her again, she could see the hope back in his eyes.

"I can probably check on him for you, if you want."

He brightened. "Yes please. He's not answering my texts."

She turned to walk back out of the room, but then she stopped. "I wasn't here when you arrived, but do you remember how difficult it was when you got here?"

"Oh, yeah. That's why I thought it would make it easier on him to have me around."

"But when you felt like shit, and everybody around you was bright and happy and doing so much better than you, how did you feel?"

Comprehension hit his gaze. "I'll give him some space. Just let him know I'm here if he needs me."

She smiled. "Bingo." She turned and exited the room, heading toward Dani's office. As she walked around the corner she spotted several people she recognized as kitchen staff inside Dani's office. She was about to turn away and come back later, but Dani caught sight of her.

"Sidney, come on in."

"I don't want to disturb you if you're busy."

"Not at all—we're finished." The group in the office made their way out, some smiling and greeting Sidney. Then Dani motioned at the seat between them and said, "Grab a chair. I was just going over the menus and the purchasing bill with the kitchen staff." She made a grimace. "Budgets— never a strong point for me."

"It must be a strong point because you keep this place running," Sidney said. "Honestly, I could never do that."

Dani laughed. "I certainly do try." She smiled at Sidney. "I hear Andrew spoke to you today."

"Yes, he did, and I think all is fine between us."

Dani nodded. "That's what I heard, too. He will be leaving here within the next twenty-four hours. He came in and signed the discharge papers after you saw him. He's pretty excited to go home."

"I suppose his bed has already been filled, ten times over?"

"It has, indeed." Dani watched her curiously for a moment. "But that's not what you're here for, so what's up?"

Dani was very observant. She didn't have any counselor or medical training, but she understood people. She was way better at that than Sidney was. "Actually, I came for an update on Cole. Brock's worried about his friend. Like, seriously worried."

"With good reason."

BROCK'S PHONE BUZZED in his hand. It was an incoming text from Cole. He smiled and settled back.

Sorry bro. Missed lunch. Trip was a bit more hazardous than I thought. Feel like shit.

Want company? he texted back.

Not today. I want to get knocked out and wake up in six months when my body no longer hurts. My heart, my mind and my soul are wanting to give in.

Sorry, Cole. Just rest. It takes a few days to adjust.

I'll need every one of those. Goodnight.

Feeling bad about his friend, but not knowing how to help him, Brock checked his schedule for the afternoon. That was one thing about being at this place, his days were pretty damn full. If it wasn't physio, it was doctors, checkups, testing, counseling, therapy, career discussions about his future and discussions about how to adapt into society with his current handicaps. That was one session he'd originally hated to go to, and now, he didn't mind at all. Everybody sat in a circle and discussed their plans for after they left this place. It gave him a chance to see how many physical handicaps everybody had. It helped him to realize he wasn't alone. He wasn't the only one struggling. Just being around different people with different mindsets was positive and helpful.

Determined to make the best of the day, he finished off his afternoon on a positive note and tried to keep up the same attitude for the next few days while Cole stayed in his room and rested. That Cole didn't want friends visiting was a little worrisome. But as he'd been pretty antisocial himself when he arrived, Brock could understand. And he honored his friend's wishes.

After three days, Brock was finally determined to stop by and see Cole. He walked down the hall to find the door shut once again. He'd walked in this direction a half a dozen times already, and it was always shut. He knocked and got no answer. He wasn't sure what to do. Cole was no longer answering his texts and didn't appear to be answering the door, either. Determined to find some answers, he walked back to the front reception desk and the manager. He'd spent enough time talking with Dani to at least know who she was but not enough to be especially friendly. He knocked on her door, and when he heard the call to enter, he pushed the door open and walked inside.

Dani looked up and smiled. "Hello, Brock."

"Hi. Do you have a moment?"

Dani set aside the file folder she was holding. "Of course. What can I do for you? And by the way, you're looking great."

He smiled self-consciously. "I'm certainly doing a lot better. I'm not there yet, but I can now see that I'll be up to going home when my time is up."

"Where is home again?" She looked up. "I should remember but with so many patients I do forget the details."

He shrugged. "It used to be California, but I don't have any family there anymore. I do have friends in Texas, though. So, I thought I might stay local."

Dani nodded, a big smile on her face. "That sounds like a wonderful idea. Maybe we'll get to see you often, even after you leave."

He wondered if that was actually a teasing note he heard in her voice. Did everyone know he was sweet on Sidney? Should he ask? He gave himself a mental shrug. No. Thankfully Dani spared him further anguish.

"What can I help you with?"

He motioned toward the spare chair. "Do you mind if I sit down?"

"Yes, of course, please sit."

He pushed the office door closed and sat. He turned

back to Dani, who had a slight frown on her face.

"Is there a problem?"

Then, he remembered the last time he'd dealt with Dani, before Sidney had come into his life. He shook his head. "No, not the way you mean. I'm actually just worried about Cole."

Enlightenment crossed her face. She folded her hands together on the desktop. "I'm sorry, I should've come and said something to you." She glanced down at the papers on her desk, then back up again and said, "Cole is in the hospital. With any luck, we're hoping he'll be up to returning to us in a couple of days."

Brock stared at her. He didn't know what to say but managed to force his mouth to work. "Is he badly hurt?"

She shook her head, and his fear subsided somewhat.

"No, but obviously he wasn't quite ready to be here."

Brock nodded. He stared out the window and felt the four walls closing in on him. "I'm so sorry for him."

"It happens. Not very often, but every once in a while, we get a doctor who signed off on a transfer a little too early. Or the new arrival thinks he's better than he really is or knows better than his medical team, and he relapses. He's not bad. But his fluids were low, and he was starting to run a fever. It was the prudent decision to put him in the hospital for a couple of days until he is stabilized again."

"Of course. Anything to keep him safe." He jumped to his feet, needing to get out. Like way the hell out. "I haven't been out on the grounds yet," he said. "But I have to admit I'd really like to get out there today."

"A day trip can be arranged. Or if all you're really looking for is a chance to get out and visit with the animals, make sure you tell somebody where you're going and give them an estimated time so if you don't come back we can come looking for you. It's better if you have somebody that can go with you."

He could feel her searching gaze, but he didn't know who he'd take with him. "I'd be happy to ask Sidney, but I'm sure her day is full." He rubbed his arms anxiously and shook his head. "I'll be fine on my own. I just need to get out."

"Understood."

He mumbled his thanks, turned and bolted from the room as if the walls were actually pressing in on him. Well, as fast as anybody with his damned legs could. He was so much better, but there were so many twinges and pains and things he couldn't do yet. Just the simplest of things, such as bending and picking stuff up off the floor was such a hardship when you didn't have the right muscles working and the right body parts in place. He'd had no idea he was looking at something like this when he was first injured. Recovery had been an eye-opener.

He shouldn't be surprised about Cole because, dammit, that man had probably pressured his doctor to release him early. And he'd probably ignored the warnings to take it easy. That was so Cole. Knowing that Brock was here would've just added to it. And Brock had been pushing him hard to try to get a spot at Hathaway because he'd been lonely. How very selfish of him.

Grateful for the break in his schedule, and feeling small, and hating that his friend had had such a setback, he made his way outside to the pasture where the horses were. The long grass was wonderful to walk in. Even just being outside in the fresh air was healing. Being on the deck was one thing, but walking or hobbling on the property itself was great. He had both crutches with him just for safety—the last thing he needed was a fall at this stage. He walked slowly down the fence line as the horses came over to check him out. The soft feel of their long noses and their beautiful, gentle eyes almost broke his heart.

He'd never had a chance to be around animals—at least, not very much. He remembered he'd also offered to volunteer downstairs at the vet clinic, but he hadn't returned—so much for a new start and helping others. Suddenly feeling like he needed to make up for his halfhearted start, and for Cole's problem, he slowly made his way back to the vet clinic. There, he set about cleaning cages and feeding animals with the help of the assistants. He could understand the terrified cat that hissed and howled and climbed to the farthest corner of his cage. He had felt like that when he got here. By the time he made his way through the cages and got to the bunny who was just content to be picked up and cuddled, he realized that was where he was now. He'd come a long way, just as these animals had too.

More settled, he headed back out to the waiting room and found Sidney chatting with the receptionist. Her face lit up when she saw him.

"Hey, I heard you were down here helping out."

He nodded. He figured everybody knew—they kept tabs on all the patients, which was fully understandable. If something went wrong, getting immediate help would be appreciated. Right now, while he was upset about Cole though, the care and attention was a little hard to escape. Still, it was Sidney, and she could come looking for him anytime.

He smiled at her. "I'm done now."

"Good. How about a swim?"

He stopped and looked at her. "That's actually a great idea. I just felt hemmed in earlier and needed to get out, so I went outside for a bit, then came back in to help with the animals, thinking that might switch my mood."

"And switch your mood, it does. It's one of the best ways to get out of a funk. So is exercise."

He gave a short laugh. "Good point. Okay, a swim it is. Then I need some food."

Sidney glanced at her watch. "A swim will take us right up to dinnertime."

"You're on." Feeling much better, he headed to his room to grab his trunks and towel. This was just about a perfect way to end a crappy afternoon.

Chapter 10

SIDNEY DIDN'T WANT Brock to think she'd been keeping an eye on him, but Dani had given her a heads-up about his feelings over Cole's setback. That was something she didn't want to see him get depressed over. Everybody was entitled to a day when they didn't feel one hundred percent. She'd had enough days like that herself. She kept an eye on him, though, going from window to window to see where he was. When she saw him heading back toward the building and then didn't come upstairs, she had called down to the receptionist and had been told he was in back helping out. Which was a perfect answer. When one was feeling lost and alone, helping somebody else who was in a worse condition was always a good way to return to center.

Sidney headed into the women's changing room and found a locker. She changed and grabbed her goggles before heading back out to the pool. This swim was something she was looking forward to. Her own muscles were feeling generally fatigued. Dealing with a lot of people on a daily basis pulled her down sometimes, too. Sometimes people got the wrong impression—that she was cold and hard. But that wasn't the way she was. Sometimes she just had to be a hard-ass to get people to do what they needed to do. At that moment, Marsha walked past, curled her lip in a sneer at her and kept going.

Sidney stopped. She wasn't going to let this low-lying, toxic situation continue. It had to stop. She spun around. "Marsha, what is your problem?"

With that Marsha froze, turned and snapped, "What's my problem? You."

Sidney shook her head. "You shouldn't have any problem with me. I didn't do anything."

"You're the one who pointed out I hadn't done my job." Her lips curved downward in a scowl. "Because I was friends with a patient."

Sidney rolled her eyes. "Do you think you're the only one who ever made that mistake? We all have. It's part of the business. You see what you want to see. You aren't always the best person to give diagnoses. We're supposed to be working as a team. We're supposed to always make assessments for each other. You're not perfect. None of us are."

Marsha frowned at her. "You didn't have to go to Dani about it."

Sidney's eyebrows shot up. "What are you talking about? I didn't go to Dani. I don't have to go to Dani. Dani somehow ends up hearing about everything anyway. I'm not a tattletale. If that's what's got your panties all twisted, then know it wasn't me." She turned and stalked off.

Sidney went to the deep end of the pool, put on her goggles and dove into the water, cutting cleanly through the surface. Her encounter with Marsha had been just enough to fuel the angry embers inside.

Pouring her frustration and anger into each stroke, she forced her body to move as fast as it could down the long lengths of the pool, flip-turning at each end and swimming back. She took a good eight laps as fast as she could before she came to a slow stop and just let the water wash around her.

Exhausted, she floated on her back and tried to catch her breath. She couldn't believe how drained she felt now. But it was a good fatigue—there was peacefulness inside. She floated for a long moment until she felt somebody come up beside her. She still didn't want to talk, so she just stayed where she was.

"You okay now?"

A wry laugh came out of her. She rolled over to look at Brock. "I guess that was a little display of temper, wasn't it?" she said calmly.

"Maybe. But maybe it was justified. The thing is, it doesn't really matter either way because you obviously needed the outlet, so you took it and you used it. You're looking better now." He reached across and stroked the few straggling hairs back off her face. "In fact, you look incredibly beautiful."

Sidney's skin tingled where he had touched her, and her eyes opened wide. "Brock, are you flirting with me?" she asked teasingly.

A wicked grin flashed across his face. "I don't know. Will it work if I do?" He swam closer. "You know if we were all alone ..."

She smiled. Inside her heart warmed and swelled. He was such a nice man. "If we were alone, it'd be a different story, is that it? Instead of flirting you'd be mocking me?"

"Hell, no," he protested. "As you know perfectly well." He drifted his thumb across her full bottom lip, stroking it gently.

She couldn't help herself. She kissed his thumb on its second pass. His eyes darkened with that slumbering look. She glanced around and saw that except for them, the entire pool area was empty. The corners of her mouth kicked up. "You know, for the moment, we are alone ..."

Instantly she was tugged forward into his arms, and his lips came down on hers. They barely treaded above the water as he kissed her with the heated passion she knew was inside him. She'd seen that same energy, that same passion for life in his workouts. Now, when it was fully focused on her ... Wow. She slipped her arms up around his neck to slide her fingers through his hair. Dimly, the sound of voices reached her ears. She went to pull away, murmuring, "Someone's coming."

Instead, he whispered, "Take a breath." He gazed deep into her eyes. Curious, she took a breath, and he sealed her lips with his own, and they sank below the water. Down, down, down.

Such a magical feeling. Underwater where no one could see them—at least, not yet. Avoiding the world around them. Just the two of them lost in each other's arms.

She succumbed to the magic of the moment.

THERE WAS A time and place for everything. This was certainly not it. But in its own way, this moment was perfect. Brock's heart and mind were fully engaged with a beautiful woman whose body was pressed tightly against his. As they floated, and rolled, and kissed and tumbled in joy, he realized just how absolutely unique the situation was, and he wanted so much more.

The need for oxygen strained at his lungs, but he didn't want to let her go. He'd happily drown, if he could do it in this togetherness. He'd breathed into her mouth, and she into his, as they exchanged kisses and the life force of the very air they'd taken with them. But like all good things, it had to end. Slowly they broke apart and floated to the surface. As each gasped for fresh air, they stared at each other in wonder, realizing something special had started. Not just started but had crossed that initial awkward series of first steps. At least, he hoped so. They were obviously physically compatible if the last few minutes were anything to go by. He couldn't wait to hold her again.

Making love was one of the most glorious things when the person in your arms was also the person in your heart.

He knew he wasn't a perfect specimen anymore, but he also didn't think in Sidney's case that was an issue. She'd spent a lot of time working with men in various stages of health and life. He didn't see the same repulsion or the same distaste in her he'd seen in other women. It was as if she didn't even recognize his shortcomings. Even though he knew that wasn't true because she was the one that always pinpointed them and then forced him to work on them. That in itself was unique.

As others made their way toward the pool and the coffee tables on the deck, they floated away from each other. He knew this was more to give an appearance of normality than anything else.

Besides, a few minutes to cool the ardor of his body was a good thing. But now there was frustration thrumming through his soul. He'd known going into that kiss it wasn't the time or place, but to think common sense might have stopped him. That would have been a shame. Yes, he wanted her. Yes, he wanted her more than he'd ever wanted another woman. Especially now.

But those few minutes had also been something he'd

never experienced before, and for the moment, he just wanted to savor her. There was no need to force his body into heavy physical exertion just to wear off the frustration eating at him. Instead, he simply floated on the surface of the water, just existing in the aftermath of such joy.

Something he had never expected to experience because he didn't even know it existed. Now that he knew, he couldn't wait for another opportunity to go there. Of course, his mind immediately set about trying to figure out how to make that happen. They both lived here. She worked here. His lips quirked at that thought. At some point, he was no longer going to be here. But he was also footloose and had no future locked down. In a way, if he wanted to pursue a relationship with Sidney, that was an option. Part of his talks with counselors was about a career. What steps he was going to have to take to return to a normal life.

The only family he had left was a sister, and they were no longer close. It was his friends he was closer to. If he thought Cole and Denton were going to settle in Texas, then he'd settle beside them in a heartbeat. He'd love for the three of them to do barbecues in the backyard over a beer, watching their toddlers play in the grass. In a way, there was just nothing better for a man like him. Of course, to have the toddlers, he had to have the mother. His heart immediately zoned in on Sidney. She'd be perfect for that role. She was caring and empathetic, and yet she was also the most kick-your-ass-when-you-were-down-because-you-needed-it   type of female he'd ever met. Strong when she needed to be and yet caring all the rest of the time. Those were qualities anybody would admire.

"Are you going to just float around?" Sidney joked.

He lifted his head and smiled. "I thought we came for a

nice, relaxing swim."

"Relaxing being the operative word here. I've already done a few laps and burned off some of that lovely energy. How about you?"

"And here I was, just enjoying the after-burn, and not wanting to burn it away." His gaze met hers in a knowing way. He watched the pink flush spread over her neck and cheeks, but she smiled.

In a low voice she said, "That's a nice way to put it." She glanced around at the other people sitting at tables. "Some tea might not be a bad idea."

"Are you okay? Are you ready to leave?" he asked. He wasn't. He'd only been in here a few minutes. But if she was leaving, then he would.

"I'm more than okay," she said in a low voice. "I'm not quite ready to leave. I'm going to float for a while. Stay with me?"

At the invitation, his heart shouted, *yes*. In a quiet voice, happy and content, he said, "Absolutely."

And he watched a smile start in the back of her stunning eyes before it broke through to her lips—and his heart.

Chapter 11

THE NEXT MORNING, Sidney glanced up as Dani walked into the physiotherapy office. "Good morning, everyone."

There was a hail of good mornings back her way.

Sidney caught Dani's eye. To make it look like she expected the meeting, she grabbed her notepad, pen and coffee and said, "Inside or outside?"

"Outside, always." With a laugh, the two women walked out of the office and proceeded through the building to the big back deck. As they approached the dining area, Dani said, "I'm going to grab a coffee. Pick a table and I'll join you."

Sidney chose her favorite far corner where the morning sun hit. There wasn't enough heat in the day yet to make it uncomfortable but just enough warmth she sat there with her face turned into the sunlight and relaxed. Really, right now, her world was pretty amazing. Aside from the whole Marsha issue, of course, but she'd weathered worse.

"Don't you look happy this morning," Dani teased as she returned with a cup of coffee and a fresh cinnamon bun.

"I don't know why I would," Sidney replied. "I didn't sleep well."

As if on cue, Dani held up two forks. Sidney grinned and grabbed one, and the two enjoyed the warm treat.

When they were done and sipping their coffees, Sidney cleared her throat.

"Am I in trouble?"

"Not any more than usual," Dani said with a chuckle.

At that, Sidney laughed out loud. "Ain't that the truth," she said dryly. "Apparently, I can get into trouble without trying."

"I did hear from Marsha. Not once, but twice. Apparently, you insulted her and upset her yesterday on your way into the pool. Then you supposedly had a lovemaking session in the pool."

Sidney's eyebrows shot up to her hairline. "Wow. All of that just from Marsha?"

"Absolutely."

"It certainly wasn't a lovemaking session, or anything indecent. However, I will confess there was a kiss exchanged. But only a kiss." Inside, Sidney winced. Marsha was correct in that it was completely unprofessional. But so was taking a simple kiss and blowing it up into something lewd and inappropriate. Did the woman hate her that much? Apparently. That was too damned bad. Maybe she could have handled the session with her and Andrew in a different way, but Sidney had just come back from school and hadn't adjusted herself. Not that that was any excuse for Marsha's poor on-the-job performance.

"That's what I assumed. How bad is the relationship between you and Marsha?" Dani asked.

"Apparently bad enough that she's coming to you with tales like that."

"She feels you've been very mean to her. That she was criticized unfairly." Dani sighed. "Of course this has to be investigated."

"I didn't mention the issue with Andrew to you as I knew I could switch up his program. I should have brought the problem to you earlier," Sidney admitted. "Maybe that would have avoided most of this."

Thinking to herself, Sidney had to wonder if she really had been that mean? She didn't think so. But if she'd hurt Marsha's feelings, then that wasn't right, either. She considered this a professional issue. Marsha had been sloppy in her work, and that wasn't acceptable. She needed to be able to take professional criticism. They all did. Not everybody was on their game one hundred percent of the time. Sometimes, it took other people's perspectives to see the truth. However, positive reinforcement was also important. She was not Marsha's supervisor. She glanced over at Dani.

"Has Shane mentioned anything to you?"

"I've already spoken to Shane. He's backed you up. He stated he took over the patient's care after agreeing with your assessment. He did speak to Marsha about it, and about her behavior toward you, but had thought it would die down. Instead, she came and made a formal complaint." Dani's smile was wry. "Of course, that gave me an opportunity to discuss her work performance."

"Of course, that was her and your right," Sidney said. "It's far better that she get a chance to air her grievance than hold it inside. Otherwise, it's going to fester and cause a very negative work environment for all of us."

At the relief crossing Dani's face, Sidney realized she'd been little worried about that. She reached across the table and patted Dani's hand. "I've been here a long time. We've weathered lots of ups and downs. This is just another one."

"I know." Dani's smile was sad. "It's always hard when it happens."

"Am I being disciplined, then?"

Dani shook her head. "No. I'm just going to ask you to add a little bit of oil to your tone when you speak with her. I've already spoken to Shane. I do have to go back and speak with Marsha again."

"As always, I'll try. Incompetence is something very hard to ignore. No matter whom it involves."

"Isn't that the truth. I will be monitoring Marsha's work for the time being, along with Shane, to make sure other patients are receiving the best standard of care."

They sat in companionable silence for a moment until Dani spoke again. "How serious is the relationship with Brock?"

At that, Sidney dropped her gaze to her hands on the table. She sighed and looked up at Dani. "I don't know. I'm not even sure what it is we're doing. In all my years of work, I have never met anyone that affected me like he has."

"Oh, I do understand that," Dani said with a sigh. "We've always held to that unwritten rule about no relationships between patients and the medical team. But that's shifting, and I guess that's my fault."

"I wouldn't place blame," Sidney said. "And I think the shift needs to happen. You're putting people with big needs up against people who have the ability to help solve those needs. We have men and we have women, many of them single and attractive, and temperaments will collide. Both positive and negative."

"So true. I guess it hasn't happened very much before."

"I think it started to happen when you expanded. Bringing in thirty extra patients and the extra fifty staff to deal with them means there are many more temperaments to come to terms with. More interactions, more friendships and relationships blossoming."

"Of course, my own world is changing in that same way." Dani's smile was mischievous. "I appear to have led the way this time."

"You are our leader." Sidney's grin was wide and happy for her friend. "You're going to have to put together a policy on staff and patient relationships, so there can be rules to follow."

"Another thing to add to my ever-growing list."

"I hear you." Sidney grinned. "I can't wait to meet Aaron, you know."

"He's all heart. I have to admit, it would have to take somebody like that in order to tolerate what I do here." She gave a wistful smile. "He'll be back after his exams next week, I believe."

Sydney smiled. "Is he on board with Hathaway House?"

Dani nodded. "He is, indeed. And looking forward to helping Stan out downstairs."

"That would be terrific when he's finished his training. But he has what, three or four years to become a veterinarian? That's a huge commitment?"

"More. Four or five I believe. He's looking forward to it, and it's lovely to see him with such purpose—passion for his future again."

Sidney watched the blush of pleasure cross her friend's face. She grabbed her hands. "I'm really happy for you, Dani. It couldn't have happened to a better person."

"What about you and Brock?" Dani asked with a laugh. "You deserve happiness, too, you know."

"Ha, we've only kissed so I don't even know what we are yet. At the risk of overthinking the situation, I have no idea what his plans are, and I've been here for a long time. I wasn't really looking to leave, yet."

Dani patted her hand gently. "I definitely hope it won't be for a while, but if it's time for a change, I would certainly understand."

"I would too. But at same time it's not where I want to see my future."

"How's Brock doing with his emotional issues?" Dani asked.

"That's actually a good question. He was very angry when we first met. That's eased a lot now. I'm not sure he's totally dealt with the problem though."

"Sometimes we deal with stuff up to a certain point, and then it takes a trigger to push us over the edge."

"The trouble is, those triggers can be damned painful."

"Absolutely. But maybe having Cole here will help."

"Actually, I'm afraid having Cole here could make it worse." Sidney didn't really have any basis for that thought, but instinct said it wasn't going to be as smooth a ride as they'd hoped.

"That's not good," Dani said. "I worked hard to bring the men together."

"So far, I think it's been a great reminder that he's lucky to be who he is and where he's is. But I know he's also really worried and, for now, until Cole's back and settled in and doing better, he's going to be very stressed and focused on his friend's return."

"Why's that bad?" Dani asked. "Particularly when you consider what some of his issues were?"

"Because he's not talking about it. This is going to allow him to transfer his anger and his hurt and whatever else is going on inside his head to this new target and let him avoid looking at his own issues."

Dani sat back with a frown. "Maybe that's something that needs to be brought up with the rest of his team?"

Staring out at the green fields and the horses in the distance, Sidney nodded. "It's something I need to do. I just haven't gotten to that point yet. I don't want to jump the gun and assume anything in terms of his treatment and his recovery. At the same time, I can see a potential problem, but as long as it's only a potential problem, then it's not something I need to bring up."

"Unless it is a potential problem that you can't stop from becoming a bigger problem without intervention."

"Decisions, decisions." She gave Dani a warm smile. "Here I am up against the same problem as Marsha, which puts me in an interesting spot. As much as I want to go and talk to the team, I don't really want it to get back to Brock that I was the one who brought it up."

"You don't want Brock to worry?"

"I don't want Brock to think I betrayed him."

"I think in this instance, it has to happen. I don't like the word betrayal, as it doesn't really convey the right meaning, but you're right. He's likely to view it that way, at least at first. I do understand what I'm asking. I think it's a professional understanding of a potential problem that could be averted if somebody would bring it up and discuss it with him. That's partly your job. If he's going to hold that against you, and I know how difficult this is, then you don't have what you think you have with him."

"Oh, I do understand that, and I have considered all of it. The trouble is that reality is a bit of a bitch. I'm not exactly sure he's ready to hear the truth on that issue."

"No, but if you were talking to any other physiotherapist right now, you know exactly what you would say."

"I know. That's why I'm talking to you. Because I know that ultimately you are going to tell me to go and do what needs to be done and not what he would like to think needs to be done."

As nights went, last night had been perfect. Brock had gone to bed with a smile on his face, and when he had woken up, the smile was still there. After all, he'd spent a fantastic hour in the pool with Sidney last night. He never expected to find somebody who mattered so much in a place like this. He'd not been against the idea. He just thought maybe professionally it wasn't the best for both parties. And even now, he wondered. He understood the problem had been with Andrew becoming friends with his physiotherapist, and that when that little bit of doubt crossed his mind, he wondered if Sidney would get in trouble for the same thing. He could see himself doing what she'd done, if the roles were reversed. Hell, everybody would want to do the best for their friend. Look at him and Cole.

At that reminder, the smile was wiped off his face. On his way to breakfast, he headed to the front room and the reception desk where he spoke to Melissa.

"Any sign of Cole coming back today?"

"Cole will be back tomorrow morning," she replied with a bright smile.

Instantly, he felt just that much better. "Thank you," he said. "That's the best news ever."

His heart lighter, he made his way out to breakfast. On the patio, he saw Sidney and Dani sitting together, clearly in intense conversation. He didn't know if something else had gone wrong, but he hoped it didn't involve him. He wanted to keep getting top-quality care, because ultimately, that was what he was here for. He wondered about the idea of having a different therapist. Or would that happen as he progressed? Would that be something that would benefit him? He didn't know. He'd been through a lot of physiotherapists before Sidney arrived. As soon as he'd met her, everything had changed for the better.

Still, a good night's sleep and a bright, cheerful morning had given him a raging appetite. The aroma of the breakfast made his stomach growl. Brock loaded his tray higher than ever, and he stared at it, feeling bemused. Then one of the kitchen staff behind the counter walked over. He picked up Brock's tray.

"I got it for you, man. You must be hungry today."

"Honestly, I'm starving," Brock replied as he led the worker to his table. He stared down at the pancakes, sausages, hash browns, toast, orange juice and coffee and smiled. This was something he could get behind.

And maybe it would help him to clear his thoughts as he started his day. His gaze lifted, and he caught sight of Sidney again. He smiled. Really, all he needed was to see her to get a better start to his day. He was a fool to worry so. He just needed to focus on the important things … and one of those was how she made him feel.

Chapter 12

THE NEXT FEW days fell into a regular pattern, and it was a pattern Sidney liked. She wanted the routine and the safety and comfort of knowing she was back where she belonged. It hadn't been an easy adjustment. Not with Marsha and Andrew. But also, a level of discomfort had developed in the relationship between her and Brock. Before, they had just been friends, but she managed to keep her own perspective. Now, for the first time, she wondered if she was being as detached as she needed to be with his care. Was she falling into the same trap Marsha had fallen into? That would be the worst. Particularly after everything she'd been through already. It was something in the back of her mind she couldn't quite let go of. Because of that, she kept her personal time with Brock as impersonal as she could. It was friendly and polite, but not loving. Maybe that was wrong of her, but she felt she needed the distance to make sure she wasn't falling down that same rabbit hole.

Maybe it was because she was afraid she worked him a little harder than she had to, but he seemed to thrive on it. There was just something about seeing a big man come back fully into his own that gave such a sense of accomplishment for both of them. After one particularly grueling session, instead of tears in his eyes, which she had seen in the past, his gaze shone with a sense of achievement. "I'm doing much better, aren't I?"

She flopped down onto the mat in front of him and laughed. "That's not the word I would use. You're doing fantastic."

Shane, who'd been working on the other side of the room, came over to talk to them. "Hey, Brock. I didn't know you had that in you."

Brock laughed, clearly a bit uncomfortable with the attention, but it was obvious to everyone he was pleased with the compliment. "Thanks. It felt like a long road to get here. I sure as hell wouldn't have made it as far and as fast without Sidney, though."

Sidney laughed. She handed Shane her clipboard.

"Are you doing anything for the next hour?"

Shane looked to his patient who was being wheeled to the pool for a therapy session with somebody else.

"Actually I have a bit of a break. I don't know about an hour, though. Why, what's up?"

"In the spirit of making sure I'm not missing anything," she said with a smile at the two of them, "is there any chance you could run through a few exercises with Brock and assess him for yourself?"

Shane's eyes lit with understanding. "You know it isn't a bad idea if we set something like this up on a regular basis."

"I was wondering that myself. I mentioned it to Dani."

"What's going on?" Brock asked.

She smiled. "I just thought that having a change of perspective on your treatment and your development, from someone who has worked with you earlier, could possibly point out something I'm not seeing."

Brock leaned forward onto the machine where he sat and said, "This is about Marsha, is it not?"

She flushed ever so slightly, heat washing over her cheeks. "Maybe, but regardless, it's a good idea."

"It's not your fault, you know." Brock grabbed the towel beside him and wiped his face and shoulders, tossing the towel over his neck. "I don't have any objection to Shane putting me through the paces. Although I'm not sure I'm up for it today, considering I'm as tired as I am, but you shouldn't let her erode your self-confidence."

Surprising herself, she blurted out, "But I eroded hers."

Both men stopped and stared at her. She shrugged. "I didn't mean to say that. I just realized how much it bothered me. She complained to Dani, so a formal investigation had to be opened." She motioned at the clipboard now in Shane's hand. "Before it comes to something and it gets any uglier, I would like you to take a look at what I've been doing, and what Brock's been doing, and see if I've missed something."

Shane nodded. "Happy to. But I don't want you to let Marsha get to you. She did miss something, but it never even crossed her mind to ask for help. At least you try to be open and honest about it, and you look for a second opinion. That's normal in our business. That's why I think we should make some changes. We all have multiple patients. There should be discussions on the best treatment for each of them between us. We aren't islands here. We should be a team on an island together."

Sidney liked that. She gave him a big, quick hug and said, "I will leave you two for the next half an hour. I'm going down to make that suggestion to Dani right now." With a bright smile, she turned and walked away.

Shane was one of the easiest people to get along with. He was always open to ideas, and he often saw where problems were that needed to be fixed before anybody else did. She really appreciated working with him. She'd grown as a physiotherapist here because of him. Sidney worried Brock had dominated her thoughts a little too much. What if she had missed something herself?

She peered into Dani's office, to find her friend on the phone and buried in paperwork. She frowned, considering whether she should walk away and come back later, but then she saw her folder was on the top of the stack and realized this needed to happen now. So, she waited.

BROCK MOTIONED AT the clipboard in Shane's hand. "I can't imagine she could possibly have done anything wrong, when I personally know how much I've improved since she took over my care."

"She's all heart. Therefore, she wants to make sure her relationship with you hasn't affected her ability to be detached enough to see what you need and don't need. I approve of what she's doing, and I certainly understand it. Because of Marsha there's been a lot of bad blood, and that's something she's very uncomfortable with, too."

He couldn't help himself. "My relationship with Sidney?"

Shane shot him a knowing look. "I know exactly what's going on between you two, regardless of all the rumors about that little lovemaking session in the pool."

Brock's heart stalled, and then raced. He opened his mouth to speak.

But Shane was still talking. "I happen to really like Sidney. I know she had a bum deal with her last boyfriend, so

I'm hoping what you're feeling is more than just a fly-by-night attraction because she's a long-term girl. She is one of those that you take home to your mom. I know that her heart is already engaged, so I'm really hoping you aren't going to mess her up."

As much as Brock loved to hear that his attraction to Sidney was reciprocated, and he already knew she was the take-home kind of girl, he was still stuck on that "lovemaking session" bit. "You do know we only shared a kiss in the pool, right?"

Shane studied him searchingly. "You serious?"

"Yes. I kissed her, but that was it. Believe me, I wanted to do more. But obviously, it wasn't the time or the place."

Shane let out a rumble of laughter. "Absolutely not the right time or place, considering somebody's passing rumors about her screwing around with you in the pool and making it sound nasty and kinky and very much something she wouldn't want other people to see."

"I'm certainly not into having other people watch," Brock said in horror. "I can't imagine Sidney would appreciate anybody passing rumors around about her."

"No, locker talk is not something any girl likes. Especially not somebody as sensitive and simple as Sidney is. She's very straightforward and honest. There will be bloodshed over this if she ever finds out."

"Then I'm presuming she doesn't know yet, or she has heard some but not the whole story."

"I assume not, too, but I don't know for sure." Shane looked back down at the clipboard. "Now, if you're up to it, I could run you through a couple of tests that will give me a good idea of where you're at."

"After what you just said, absolutely. I feel like I need to pound something into the ground, but I'll take it out on the equipment, not my body, then a little bit out on Marsha."

"Relax about her. That kind of behavior always has fallout. She'll get her own. You don't have to do anything about it." Shane dropped the clipboard and turned to look at him. "Just so we understand each other—it would be much worse for Sidney if you did try to defend her."

Brock clenched his jaw and glared at Shane. He understood what Shane was saying, but it was going to be damned hard to let anybody else say something nasty about Sidney.

"Brock, do you understand me? If you make this a big deal, it's only going to get worse. Dani won't have much of a choice but to step in hard. Do you understand that?"

"Yes," he bit off. "But it's not fair. Sidney didn't do anything." His glare deepened. "Neither did I. That's just as upsetting as thinking somebody is attacking her. It's also my honor."

"I hear you. So let's get to work and make sure there is nothing here that Sidney can be held accountable for."

On that note, Brock gave him a hard nod. "Where do we start?"

Chapter 13

D ANI LOOKED UP as she replaced the phone on her desk and smiled at Sidney. "I was just about to call you."

"Oh, good. I came because Shane and I were discussing some of the issues between physiotherapists and patients and friendships. We were thinking that as a common practice, we should check in on each other's patients—just to get a new perspective, a second professional opinion." Sidney exhaled, realizing she was babbling. But her employee file had been open on Dani's desk.

Dani's eyebrows rose. "This is because of Marsha?"

"Shane asked me the same thing. In a way, yes, it is, because it did illustrate the fact that we have a flaw in the system. Nobody else had seen her work, and in the work she did with Andrew, there was either a mistake or simply poor work being done. If another physiotherapist had been working with Marsha, it would be quite likely problems would have been noticed sooner. But she did the bulk of the work with him exclusively."

"You're saying that the team system we have in place isn't enough?" Dani asked as she leaned forward and propped her elbows on the desk, studying Sidney.

"I do think the team system works well," Sidney said. "But I think we need more team-based physiotherapy relationships as well."

"So, you're suggesting doubling up on each patient?"

The frown was almost instant, and in that moment Sidney shook her head and smiled. "No, no. I'm not talking about needing to have twice as many physiotherapists or booking in twice as much time with each patient. I can certainly understand the budget being your primary concern."

"It's not that it's a primary concern, but it's definitely a constant concern so if you're suggesting we need to do something like that, the budget just does not allow for it as it stands."

Sidney shook her head again. "That's not what I'm saying at all. I'm just saying that in the days and weeks that we plan out our work with each patient, we need to have somebody come by on a regular basis to see how things are working out and to give a professional second opinion. Honestly, it's no big deal. It's just something that Marsha, and now my relationship with Brock, has brought to the forefront."

"Is it something I need to set up, or is this something you need to set up?" Dani sat back.

Feeling better about the whole situation, Sidney said, "It's really something that we physiotherapists can do between us ourselves, maybe with Shane taking the lead on it. I just wanted to run the idea past you."

"Consider the idea run, and I approve. Anything that helps to improve patient care is the bottom line."

"I figured that's how you'd feel, and I'm quite glad, actually. Shane is currently putting Brock through a couple of exercises to see how he's doing. I wouldn't want to think my own feelings had gotten in the way of Brock getting the best care here he can get."

"I understand your concern, particularly with what happened with Marsha, and I guess it's certainly possible, so thank you for getting Shane to step in and take a look. Having brought up your relationship with Brock, maybe I can bring up something else."

"Sure." Sidney settled back in her chair, feeling much more relieved about the entire situation. She wondered if Dani was going to ask about their future, and she really didn't have too many answers for her, but she didn't want to leave the center if it wasn't necessary. If Brock decided to stay locally, she could continue to work here, and she'd be a happy camper. But she had to understand that maybe Brock needed to move elsewhere. If that was the case, then she had to consider her options, too. She had certainly left enough times and come back, but what she didn't want to do was leave for a relationship that was going to end, and then come back.

It would really suck to leave with her boyfriend, and then find out that it wasn't what she thought it was.

"I told you about Marsha and the pool."

"Right. The famous kiss." Sidney grimaced. "Who thought that such a simple thing would make me notorious here?"

"Unfortunately, apparently Marsha didn't tell just me." Dani spoke slowly, but her gaze was direct and her tone firm. "It seems like she may have enhanced the story, and she appears to be spreading it in buckets."

Sidney stared at her, stunned. "Why?"

"I don't know for certain, but my guess is it's probably because of what you did about Andrew."

Sidney slumped in her seat. "This is why I don't have many girlfriends," she said. "That's just not something I could ever see myself doing. I might be pissed off at myself for having not done as good a job as I could, and I might be pissed off if somebody else pointed it out to me. But I'm sure as hell not going to blame the other person and go so far as to get revenge."

"That's why we *are* friends," Dani said with a brilliant smile. "I can't do that to anyone either. But we do know that not everybody thinks or acts the way we do. Right now, I have a situation on my hands that I have never had to face before."

"I just gave her more fodder, didn't I?"

That startled a laugh out of Dani, and she leaned forward conspiratorially. "That said, it was a good kiss, right?" Her eyebrows rose and fell suggestively.

Sidney giggled. "Oh, my God, it so was."

Then she collapsed in big, boisterous gales of laughter. No matter what happened with Marsha, Brock was in her life. She didn't know where that was going to take them, but she wanted to give it as much of a chance as she could. "Too bad there isn't any way to prove what happened."

"Actually, there is. People tend to forget I have security cameras everywhere in this place."

Sidney gasped, heat flushing over her cheeks. "Now that could have been embarrassing."

Dani looked at her with a sideways smile. "This is where we go back to that question—is there anything I'm going to find on that tape other than a kiss?"

"No. But let me tell you, it was *some* kiss."

"Having brought it to the head that she has, I don't have any choice but to view it to make sure I understand exactly what went on and when," Dani said. "Then I will have to deal with Marsha."

"I'm sorry about that. It never occurred to me somebody would have that kind of vindictiveness. She's right, though. We shouldn't have kissed like that." She leaned her head back and stared up at the ceiling of Dani's office. Not as passionate a kiss, at least. She frowned. It looked like the situation was far from over.

IT WAS LATE in the afternoon when Brock made his way to his bed. He hadn't had to use crutches for a long time, but his left leg was cramping, and he felt weak today. It was a setback he wasn't impressed with. He'd been walking pretty decently, with a limp and one crutch under his left arm, but still managing to mimic a fairly natural movement. However, today he was dragging that damned lame foot. He understood progress came in stages. He also understood, from the team meetings, how much mental processes affected the healing ability of the body. All that was fine in theory, but it was a different story when you were dealing with a setback. Resting the crutches along the bottom of the bed, he lay down with a sigh. It was such a relief to get his sore leg up. For the first time in a long time, he wondered if maybe he should just have dinner in.

He wasn't sure what had gone wrong, but today he just felt like crap. Had the extra testing with Shane worn him down that much more? Maybe that was all it was—just a bad afternoon. Who knew? He'd read all kinds of journals about diet affecting healing and joints and what not, but he wondered how it was possible to learn to do everything. He suddenly felt disappointed with where he was at the moment. He certainly couldn't blame Shane because the things he'd had him do hadn't been that strenuous. The only good thing about today was the fact Shane was pleased with his progress. And Shane would know, since they'd worked together earlier, prior to Sidney's arrival.

"Brock, you've come a long way," Shane had said with an encouraging nod. "You can put the success for that squarely on Sidney and yourself."

"So," Brock had asked in a low tone, checking to make sure nobody else was close enough to overhear him, "Sidney didn't pull a Marsha, then?"

Shane had smiled, patted him on the shoulder and said, "Sidney pulled a Sidney. Behaving as she always does—as a consummate professional. That she's also allowed herself to open up to something more between the two of you just makes her very special."

"Could she get in trouble for that?"

"That's a little harder to determine." Shane looked at him knowingly. "Maybe keep the little swimming pool scenarios out of the relationship for now. Actually, out of all public places."

"That leaves nowhere else," Brock said. "But I would never want to do anything to jeopardize her position, or her professional reputation."

"Both have been hit lately."

The conversation had dwindled after that.

Now Brock stared at the bedroom door. Privacy with Sidney? Today it seemed like a long way away. It wasn't, but as he'd had a physical setback, he was pretty darned sure she'd had a setback in this place, and for that, he felt guilty as hell. If only he had more energy to make his way down to Dani's to give an explanation. Not that there was much to be said. He wanted Sidney and had reached out and taken just a tiny delight in that kiss. He was sorry somebody had seen them. Sorry something so beautiful had become degraded. Determined to set things right, he reached for his phone and found Dani in the contacts. He hit dial and collapsed back onto the bed with the phone to his ear, waiting for her to pick up. Finally he heard a cheerful voice on the end of the phone.

"Hi, Dani. It's Brock. Can you come to my room for a moment?"

"Sure can. I'll be down in five."

Brock lay with the phone at his side and waited for her to walk down the hallway. He recognized Dani's footsteps as soon as she got close.

At the door, she knocked and then entered. She saw him and she said, "Oh dear."

He gave a half laugh and motioned her inside. "I'm fine. Just not as good a day as some days."

She nodded her head in commiseration. "That happens. Even for those of us that aren't injured."

"So true." He remembered those days well. One tried to be upbeat and happy, but there were just some days when you got out of bed and everything seemed like shit. "Thank you for coming."

"I'm always happy to see you. What can I do for you?"

"A couple of things. I understand Cole's return was delayed yet again. He will be coming back, won't he?" he asked hopefully.

She smiled. "Absolutely. I'm expecting him tomorrow morning."

He gave a heartfelt sigh of relief. "I've been very worried about him."

"We all were. We will take his adjustment slow."

At those words, Brock studied Dani with a wry smile. "Good luck with that."

"That's a very perceptive comment." She laughed. "We see it a lot. Everybody has their standards of what they think they should be doing, but the body is completely disconnected from that expectation. It will do things in the timeframe acceptable to it. That's often difficult for people to accept."

"Like me." He stared down at his leg. "Progress has been phenomenal," he said. "But after all this talk about Sidney, I was getting disturbed."

"Oh dear, I'm sorry to hear that. Rumors are always something we try to stop, but it's not possible. Not when there are more than two people around." She pulled his chair over and sat down next to the bed. "What is it about Marsha's situation that bothered you?"

"It actually made me concerned Sidney was doing the same thing—with me. Overlooking important signs that would impact my progress." There. He had brought out the relationship between him and Sidney for the first time.

Obviously she knew because she nodded. "It's a valid point. It would never be a good thing to have your confidence in a professional team around you eroded because of something like that." She paused. "Are you asking for a new therapist?"

"Oh, no. No." He shook his head. "You're misunderstanding. Actually, I was going to talk to Sidney about it, but she brought it up herself this morning at our session. Shane was there, working, and she called him over and asked him if he could take a look at me running through some exercises and some tests to see if she had missed something."

Dani's eyebrows rose in surprise. "Now that's very interesting."

"I was quite surprised, too, however, as I had already been wondering if it's something I should've brought up with her, I was actually very happy to have her bring it up for me."

"How did Shane how feel about it?"

"He asked if this had anything to do with Marsha."

Dani's face clouded over. "It is amazing how one incident can permeate a professional culture and cause trouble."

"He was happy to do it. He did tell her it wasn't necessary, but she said she would like him to do it because *she* felt it was necessary."

"I'm very glad you told me about this," Dani said. "Are you happy with the diagnosis Shane gave you?"

Brock grinned. "He said Sidney was doing a damned good job. There were no concerns."

At that, Dani laughed. "Yes, that's what we like to hear." She stood as if to leave.

"I don't want to get Sidney into trouble," Brock said. "So please don't tell her I told you what happened."

Dani looked down at him, but there was a gentle smile on her face. "That's the thing about Sidney—she's a professional through and through. She already came to me and told me she asked Shane to spend some time with you, going over what she'd been doing."

At the look of relief crossing Brock's face, she laughed. "We try to be a family here. Some members of the family are willing to do what is necessary." She walked toward the door. "Sidney suggested there needs to be checks and balances between the physiotherapists. Something they should carry out amongst themselves on every patient." She turned to look back at Brock. "So, thank you. It's nice to know the team is developing better ways to serve everyone." With that, she turned to the door.

"Wait," he called out.

Dani turned, a questioning look on her face. "I'm sorry, I didn't even ask if there was anything else bothering you."

He motioned at the door. "Could you close it? What I have to say next is a little private."

Dani closed the bedroom door and came back toward him. "You've been worrying over lots of problems. Feel free to talk to me anytime."

"I know. I just realized this has become a bigger issue." He took a deep breath. "I want to apologize."

The faintest frown crossed Dani's face. "Why would you have anything to apologize for?"

"The kiss in the pool."

He could see the understanding dawn on her face. He hurried on, wanting to get the words out.

"I also understand other people saw us." He shook his head. "I thought for sure nobody was around. I never considered the position it would put Sidney in." He swallowed hard. "I have to admit, given the same circumstances, it would be damned hard to not do the same thing. I'm really falling for her. It's just that given the circumstances I crossed the line."

"Did she push you away?" Dani asked, her voice serious but a smile playing at the corner of her lips.

"No, she didn't. She responded wonderfully."

Dani's smile widened.

"Moreover, I couldn't have expected what would happen."

"We do know it won't happen again in such a public place, don't we?" she asked.

He grinned, realizing that apparently this wasn't such a

big deal. "I would hope not."

"So then you have nothing to apologize for because if Sidney responded, then she was not upset either. Now, if you had forced her, then that would be different."

"She definitely wasn't unwilling." He gave her a lopsided grin. "And for that I'm incredibly grateful."

Dani laughed—a beautiful, chiming sound that rang around the room. "That something so beautiful can happen between you and Sidney is awesome. It was after work hours, it was on your own time. It was in the pool where somebody saw you, and that is unfortunate. In most cases, it wouldn't be a problem. However, the person who saw you holds a grudge against Sidney, so things became nastier than they should have."

"Marsha?" He'd already heard from Shane, but Dani confirmed it.

Dani nodded. "But you don't have to worry, I will deal with it. Now, was there anything else bothering you?"

Her tone was teasing, and he took no offense. He'd like to think they were moving past the formalities to friendship. He'd been here long enough now he considered many of the people here friends. Of course, he considered Sidney a whole lot more, but as these people were her friends he didn't want to alienate anyone. He shook his head. "I think that empties all the bits and pieces bugging me."

Dani stood up. "Good, because healing will not happen while all of those issues are festering. So I'm glad you felt free enough to tell me about you and Sidney. As Sidney's my friend, I'm delighted for her." She gave him a big wink, turned and walked out, leaving Brock grinning like a fool.

He collapsed back with a smile on his face. So everything he thought about Sidney was true. His confidence, although slightly eroded by Marsha's comments, went up.

He glanced down at his leg, realizing the throbbing had stopped, and although it was sorer than he had expected, his mood and spirits were up, and he was no longer feeling such a heavy burden. In fact, he was seriously thinking of a swim and shower before dinner. He desperately wanted to meet up with Sidney for dinner.

Chapter 14

S IDNEY STOOD AT the entrance to the big, open dining room and studied the noisy population already in residence. The last thing she really wanted at this point was more people. She definitely didn't want to have anything to do with the physiotherapists she worked with, one of them in particular. She was feeling very anti-people this evening. As she glanced outside at the late-afternoon sunshine and the green grass, she thought about what she really wanted.

"Sidney, what can I get you today?"

She smiled at Dennis, one of the guys working on the other side of the counter, and said, "Do you have anything to take out? I just want to get outside onto the grass, maybe sit in the pasture with the horses."

Dennis's face burst into a big grin. "You want a picnic? That's awesome." He glanced up and down the line of hot, steaming trays already out. "Is there anything here in particular you're looking at for dinner?" he said. "I can pack it up for you. You can just bring the containers back to be washed."

"Thank you. It all looks wonderful. But something that's easy to eat would be better."

Dennis pointed at the beef bourguignon. "How about a main dish of that, and a big green salad?"

"I don't know how easy it would be to eat but it looks

delicious, so yes. Thanks." She studied the desserts and said, "I'll come back for coffee and dessert afterward."

"Give me five." Dennis disappeared into the kitchen. While she waited, Sidney picked up a bottle of water to go with her dinner. Dessert was going to be a piece of divine-looking chocolate cake.

Dennis returned a few moments later with a plastic bag. He came around the buffet and opened it up to show her. Inside were a knife and a fork, and two very large containers.

"Wow, that's a lot of food."

"You can eat. I've been serving you for years. I know this is probably just round one for you."

She laughed and added her bottle of water to the bag. She thanked Dennis, then turned and headed downstairs, stopping in at the vet's to say hi to Stan on her way out.

"Did anybody else come to visit today?" she asked him.

"Dani's out in the pasture. She's brought in a new horse—an old mare heading for the glue factory."

"Perfect, I brought a picnic dinner and I was going to head out to the pasture. Where is she?"

"She's in the same pasture with Molly and Maggie. All three of them are getting along just fine."

"I haven't visited with little Molly in a while," Sidney said. She could sense Stan studying her face. She gave him a smile. "I'm fine. Honestly. I just need a bit of food and fresh air."

"You always know you're welcome down here," he said. "If you want company, I'll bring out coffee in a little while."

"I'd like that. Thanks." She grabbed her bag and headed out back. Heading out through the corral system was the easiest and fastest way to get to the pastures.

Of course, almost as if they knew she was coming, Maggie and baby Molly had made their way to the fence, a big silver dapple mare behind them. But there was no sign of Dani. Sidney'd forgotten to ask Stan what the new horse's name was. She walked over and hopped up onto the corner fence to give them each a big cuddle, and then she pulled out her hot dish. It had cooled somewhat, but now it was the perfect eating temperature. With the sun shining on her face, and the animals surrounding her and the whole of Hathaway House behind her, she dug in to enjoy her dinner.

IGNORING THE WEAKNESS in his leg, Brock proceeded toward the dining room. He stood at the entrance and studied the big open room. There were a good fifty to sixty people sitting down and eating, the rumble of conversation bright and cheerful. Not at all what he wanted. He studied the faces, recognizing a lot of the people he'd come to know. There were a lot of good people here. But although he tried, he couldn't find Sidney.

He pulled his phone out and sent her a text. **Where are you?**

The response surprised him. **Out in the paddock with the horses. I brought dinner out here.**

He studied the phone in his hand, and a slow smile came over his face. A picnic. What a great idea. Could he join her, though? What Sidney was allowed versus what he was allowed was the difference between employee and patient, but it was worth a try. She had told him where she was, so maybe that was already an invitation? He figured there were enough problems that he was much better off giving her a chance to say no. Then he stopped with that thought. What if she wasn't being honest? He shook his head, feeling like a dithering fool.

At that moment, Dennis walked over. "Hey, what can I get you tonight?"

Brock raised his gaze to the other man and smiled. "I'm just trying to figure that out."

His phone rang just then. He excused himself and answered the call.

"Hey Brock," Sidney said. "When I said I was out by the horses, I meant it. I actually had Dennis pack me several containers and am sitting out here having dinner."

"That sounds wonderful. Are you interested in company?" He tried to keep his tone neutral.

"Absolutely. Come down to the vet's, and then head out along the hall toward the horse stalls. You'll see me there."

He ended the call and turned to face Dennis. "A little bird told me you packed a picnic for her. Any chance I could get the same for myself?"

Dennis flashed him a wicked grin. "Are you going to take it to eat with her?"

"Absolutely."

Dennis laughed. "Good for you. In that case, tell me what you want, and I will pull it together."

That was easy enough. Brock walked along the counter, hearing his stomach start to growl. His energy was picking up at the thought of food, too. He was no longer anywhere near as tired as he had been. He ordered a decent-sized dinner, and before long, Dennis was standing beside him with all of the food packed up in glass containers. He handed the bag over.

"Here. Just make sure you bring all the containers back so we can get them washed up for tomorrow."

"Awesome." Brock glanced at the coffee and desserts and said, "I guess I can come back for the second course?"

"Exactly what Sidney said."

With conspiratorial grins the two men parted ways, and Brock headed down to the vet's office. The elevator opened up on the vet's level, and he took a left down the hallway toward the horses. He didn't want to waste any time in conversation with the others, so he headed straight outside.

As he walked out into the sunshine, he blinked at the bright light. It took him a moment to find where Sidney was. But then he saw her. She was at the corner of one of the pens, sitting on top of the railing, eating—the horses stood right beside her.

"What a perfect idea."

She laughed, her voice happily trailing across the open air. "I just couldn't stand to be inside anymore. Walls were closing in on me, and there were too many people."

"I had the same thought looking at how jam-packed it was. Even though the atmosphere seemed happy, it just felt too confining."

"Exactly. And Dennis was a sweetheart." She nodded at the bag in his hand. "Apparently, he did the same for you."

Brock hobbled closer. "Yes he did. I probably have ten times more food than you do."

"Good. Then I can share yours." She grinned at the look of bemusement on his face.

He studied the railing and frowned. "I sure would like to sit down on the top, though."

She glanced at his leg and at the logs. "I could shuffle over, and you can have the center seat at the corner here."

He hated to make her move for anything that would show him as less than capable, but the last thing he wanted was to end up falling and causing his glass containers to shatter all around them. That would be a little more embarrassing than accepting her offer to move.

He handed her up the bag, and then, laying his crutch against the railing, he swung himself up to the top of the fence post. Sitting straddled, with his back leaning against the fence to support himself, he settled in. With a big smile, he reached out a hand to Maggie, who'd walked over to check out his arrival. She gently nuzzled his hand, giving a tiny nicker.

"She's beautiful, isn't she?"

"They all are," she said quietly. "I just love the animals here. Every time I get upset or sad or lonely, I can come here and know they accept all without judgment. They are really beautiful to have around and to be available to hug and hold."

"You've had a couple of rough weeks, haven't you?"

"So have you," she tossed back. "But Cole will be back tomorrow, so that should help."

"It'll be nice to see him again," Brock admitted. "But I have a different understanding now. I get that he tried to do too much too fast, and the traveling and adjustment were something that set him back. As I've had setbacks of my own, I will do a lot to encourage him to not go that way again."

"The opposite effect can happen, just because of that," Sidney said softly. "Sometimes, we nurture people too much, and then they don't strive for more. It's important to do what you can, so your body will allow you to do more without causing injury or stress. Internal tension is just as bad as external. All the applied forces should be even. That's very hard to attain or maintain."

"Very philosophical."

Sidney looked off across the green hills. "Well, for the first time ever, I was looking at quitting."

He stared at her in surprise. "Because of Marsha? Please don't let her upset you to that extent."

"It's a lot of things. It's Marsha. It's crossing a professional line. It was getting caught and having somebody spread gossip. It just leaves a bad taste in my mouth."

"It can and likely will happen anywhere. Not just here."

She nodded. "True, but for the first time, I guess I'm open to the idea of leaving. This was always my place to work. I felt at home here and that everybody here was part of my family. It just feels odd now."

"You've really only just arrived, still haven't had time to properly adjust, and you're ready to leave? What's it been, a month? Six weeks?"

She nodded. "About that."

"It's not enough time. You've just barely settled in, and yes, some trouble started."

"It's more than that. I also have to think of my future. What is it I want to do in ten years?"

"I thought you told me this is where you want to be in ten years."

"True, but what if I want a family in the future? How do I handle that?"

"Don't most of the doctors and nurses and patients and staff here have families and relationships?"

She appeared to mull that over for a minute, then nodded. "I guess they do. For some reason, I was thinking I was going to have to leave in order to have a future."

That jolted him into silence. So, did that mean he wasn't anything she wanted in her future? He stared down at the food in his lap, and it suddenly tasted like sawdust. He took a deep breath. He had to know the answer. "Does that mean you're not interested in a relationship with me?"

She spun and looked at him. "No, that's not what I meant at all. Why would you think that?"

"Because you just said you would have to leave to find your future."

She stared at him, her eyes round, and then she frowned. "Because you're going to leave."

"Am I?" He tilted his head and studied her. Looking for some truth on the inside that would tell him they were both heading to the same place. "I can work in Dallas as well as I can work anywhere."

"What work?" she asked with curiosity. "I don't think we've ever discussed that."

"That's because so many people think when you're a military grunt that's all you are, but I'm actually very good with computers. I'm sure I could get an IT job in the big city."

"Won't you need more training?"

He shook his head and smiled. "No. This is what I did in the military."

Understanding flaring in her eyes, she said, "In that case, that would be perfect for you. Dallas is a massive city. I'm sure you'd have no trouble getting a job."

As she said that, their eyes met and held. Heat flashed at that sudden knowing they were on the same page. They were skirting around major issues, looking to see how closely their lives might fit together. He started to lean forward, seeing her stretching toward him. Just before their lips touched, the door to the vet clinic slammed open.

"Hey, Sidney?"

They broke apart and turned to face Stan.

"There you are." He ambled toward them, two big mugs of coffee in his hand. "Hey, Brock. I didn't know you were here or I'd have brought another cup."

Brock smiled at the friendly doctor. He was a man he'd be happy to call a friend. He was a good-hearted soul. A flash of relief glimmered through him that Stan didn't have any interest in Sidney on a personal level because he really wasn't up for a competition.

Brock held up the dish in his hand. "I'm still eating— not quite ready for coffee yet, thanks."

Stan handed Sidney a cup. "This is a great idea, you guys. I should do this myself. Sometimes it's just nice to come out and enjoy the sunshine."

"Isn't that the truth?" Sidney said with a smile.

Maggie trotted a few steps closer to come and see Stan. He reached through the fence post to give her a good scratch. Brock watched as Stan interacted with the horses, seeing that same natural affinity and an innate joy to be one with the animals.

"You have a special relationship with the animals and a very special place to work here," Brock said. "Not only are you working with the animals all day long but when you take a break, you naturally come out to visit and socialize with them as well."

"Actually, it's often a lot nicer," Stan said with a smile. "The reason they are in my place is because they're hurting and need help in some way or another." He patted Maggie on the nose. "These guys are all in good shape—fit, happy, healthy and enjoying life. Sometimes it helps to get away from the pain and come and see the joy."

He glanced up at Brock and added, "The same goes for

you two. You're dealing with your own pain. Sidney's dealing with the pain of a lot of people. Coming out here is all about renewal."

Brock smiled warmly. "We all need that."

Chapter 15

S IDNEY AGREED WITH both men. In fact, that was exactly what she was here for. It wasn't that she wanted to move, it was just that the first upset of returning home again had disrupted her life so badly. It was honestly the first professional dispute she'd had since she first came here. Then again, she may have avoided a lot of drama by her frequent absences for school. There were a lot of people here, along with a lot of personalities. She had to remember that fact. And if she was staying, she'd have to find a way to get along with Marsha. At the same time, it also took a lot of pressure off her shoulders to think maybe she wasn't going to have to leave.

With that thought, the grass suddenly seemed greener, and the sun a whole lot brighter. She realized the thought of leaving was more difficult than she'd imagined. She would've made peace with it, but it wasn't necessary, and therefore, Marsha was not going to be allowed to be an excuse. That meant she had to make peace with the situation somehow.

When the three of them had finished the food and drink, they walked back into the vet's office and spent the next half hour cuddling the animals. She picked one up, hugged and kissed and cuddled it a couple times, then put it back down again and picked up the next. It just went with part of her mood. After they were done, she and Brock made their way upstairs to the kitchen to return their dishes. Dennis saw them coming, and his face broke out into a big grin. They handed over the leftover containers and thanked the man profusely.

His merry laughter rolled through the big room, which was almost empty now. "It was a great idea. If you want to do it again, just let me know."

Sidney no longer wanted a coffee, but she definitely wanted dessert. Brock was likely to want some, too, so they moved down to the dessert table where Brock picked up a piece of the chocolate cake she'd been eyeing earlier and a coffee. They walked back out on the deck and into the mellowing, early-evening sunshine. As she sat there at the empty table, her face lifted to the setting sun, she realized just how absolutely perfect this place was.

"You look like you're feeling better," Brock said.

"I am. I just had to make peace with a few issues. It's stupid to let something small ruin something so important to me."

"Marsha and this place?"

She nodded. "Of course, it helps to know you might be staying close, too." She shot him a teasing glance. "Apparently, privacy around this place doesn't exist."

He laughed. "I see that. It might be easier if people know we are an item."

She nodded. "It might."

"Are we an item?"

She turned to look at him, her eyes flashing with delight.

"Are you asking me?" she teased. "Aren't you going to be a macho male and make it a fact?"

Something in his eye glinted. "Who, me?"

She chuckled. "I get it, I'm just teasing. You don't need

to be tough, here. But I'm pretty sure that's not a big part of your personality anyway."

"Well, I used to be tough. I just don't know that I still am. Maybe, but I don't really feel like it. Once I get back on my feet and into independent living, things might change. Who knows? On the other hand, a lot of who I am here is a result of all that's gone before. I'm different now. Better."

She looked over at him and smiled a slow, gentle smile. "I'm really glad I'm with this person here. Too often there are layers to our individual personalities we never let anybody else see. It's only through struggle that we get to see the inner person. I really admire and respect the man I've met here."

"Damn. I do feel like I need to confess, though. Because after all that kiss and your stuff, I did start to wonder if I should be asking for another therapist."

Silence.

"I guess that's normal," she said in a low voice.

"I didn't ask. You brought it up before I had a chance to. I was going to talk to you about it first to see if you felt it was an issue. But then when you asked Shane to look after me, I realized that you'd already considered the issue."

"What did he say about your care?" Her gaze focused on him. "It's been a hell of a day, if I forgot that."

"It has been a hell of a day. But he was very happy. He said that—you'd been your usual self—a consummate professional."

Heat flashed up her neck with pleasure as she heard his words. "I'm glad to hear that. But I also went to Dani and had a talk with her about it. I suggested all the therapists should do some round-robin checking up on patients, just to see how they are doing. It makes sense. We're all going to have a different view of each injury and how to proceed."

"Yes, Dani told me."

Sidney sat back in her chair. This whole situation was snowballing. Not only were other patients second-guessing their own therapists, but some of them had gone to Dani with their questions and concerns. She sighed. She was going to have to talk to Marsha one of these days. At that moment, Marsha walked into the dining room. She caught sight of Brock and Sidney and froze.

Shit. It looked like that future conversation was about to happen now.

Sidney glanced at Brock to see if he had noticed Marsha's arrival. "You might want to go to your room. I don't know if Marsha's looking for a fight, or what." She sighed and added, "I do need to talk to her."

Brock studied her face, turned to look at Marsha and said, "I'll stay right here, thanks."

She winced. "I really don't need an audience."

"And yet, you might. Maybe with a witness, the truth will come out."

She studied his face and nodded gratefully. "Good point."

Her heart started to pound inside her chest. She was so very non-confrontational. Yet, she was also the one known for calling a spade a spade. She wondered for a moment if there was even a chance Marsha would just brush it off, but when she glanced at Marsha again, the woman was stomping in their direction. Before Sidney could take one more breath, Marsha was already standing in front of her, hands on her hips.

"So, there you are."

Sidney straightened in the chair. "Yes, I'm here, did you

want me for something?"

"I've reported you're fraternizing with a patient to Dani."

"Fraternizing? Interesting phrase." She smiled at Brock and said, "If you mean the friendship developing between Brock and me, that's fine. Dani already knows."

Marsha's lips thinned. "So, it's okay for you to be friends with a patient but not for me?"

"It's okay for all of us to be friends with patients," Sidney said. "It's not okay when that friendship affects how we do our job."

Marsha's lips turned into a sneer. "So, of course, you haven't had any problems being detached in your work with Brock?"

Sidney barked out a short laugh. "Of course, you're perfectly right. I'm not perfect. I'm not detached. When you care about somebody, you can't be detached. However, as professionals, it's our job to do the best we can, and when we can't, we need to rely on others and ask them to help out."

"That's not likely to happen." Marsha shook her head. "It appears you have the complete run of this place."

"I'm sorry you feel that way. I was hoping we could find a decent working relationship moving forward."

"It's got to be you or me," Marsha said. "There's no way in hell I am working with you."

Sidney nodded wearily. "Again, I'm sorry to hear that, and I wish you luck with finding another job. You're very talented—I'm sure there's lots of places that would be happy to hire you."

Marsha looked at her, nonplussed. "I'm talented?" She shook her head. "How does that fit in with everything else you said about me?"

"I said nothing about you. I told you that you weren't being detached and had missed seeing some things that needed to be seen. All you had to do was ask somebody else to see if your perspective was skewed because of the relationship."

"Oh, sure. It's not like you've ever done that."

Sidney was damned happy to reply to the woman's accusation. "Yes, in fact, I have." She motioned at Brock. "I had Shane run Brock through the paces, to see what I might've missed." She paused. "For that matter, moving forward, that is going to become common practice between all of us. To be discussed at tomorrow's meeting. It has already been cleared with Dani."

"What's going to be common practice?"

"More teamwork. Having another therapist see how the work is going, so it's not just one person's prognosis, because each of us sees progress in a different way."

Marsha's face was an interesting play of emotions. It was as if she liked the idea, but she didn't want to like the idea.

"Oh."

"Every time something like this happens, we have to learn from it," Sidney said. "I didn't expect to have a friendship with Brock, but once I did, I realized I hadn't really understood what you were up against."

"I wasn't Andrew's lover," Marsha sneered.

"That's good because Andrew is happily married. However, Brock is not, and I'm not his lover, either."

"Oh?" Marsha's face was a study of consternation as she looked between Brock—who was sitting back, quietly watching the two of them—and Sidney. "But I saw you in the pool?"

"Absolutely, you saw a kiss between two people who are

fond of each other. Between people who are looking to have a relationship, and who were caught by surprise at just how much there was already between us," Sidney admitted. "A kiss that was probably too passionate, but it was past work hours, and I was not on the clock. It was our own personal time, in a pool we are entitled to be in. I'd have preferred nobody saw us, of course. But I would have also preferred those that saw us would not have tattled or severely embellished the story out of malice. You also have to understand Dani has security feeds all over that area. So of course, she checked out the videos to see for herself what happened."

"Oh," Marsha said in a small voice. "I didn't know that."

"In the many years Dani's been running this place, she's been up against almost every possible scenario between two people. When she runs a complex of this magnitude, with hundreds of people—employees, patients and visiting staff, not to mention all the support staff—including the veterinarian clinic—she needs to know what is happening."

Sidney had no idea how Brock was feeling about all of this, but she didn't dare take her gaze off Marsha. She had to get this all out and dealt with now. "All Dani expects from us is a professional environment at all times while on duty. Our private lives are, as always, our own."

She stood, towering way above Marsha. She didn't intend it is a power play, but she wanted to let her know exactly what she needed from her. "That's what I would like to see. My private life is my life, and you're entitled to yours. If it doesn't cross the line in terms of patient care, it's neither of our business. As for that mistake, hopefully this new system will prevent it from happening again because I don't believe you did it on purpose. I just think it was one of those blind spots that can creep up on us when our focus is elsewhere."

Marsha nodded. "I didn't do it on purpose. I wouldn't hurt Andrew. Of course, I wanted to give him the best care possible. I won't do it again."

"I'm certain you won't," Sidney said warmly. "But at the same time, the way you dealt with the problem and the way you've dealt with me since is not something I'm happy with."

Marsha looked very uncomfortable. Clearly, she'd come over intending to blast Sidney and make a few demands of her own. Now she was in the hot seat, and it was not a very nice place to be. Sidney took pity on her.

"If possible, I'd like to put this behind us and move forward as the two professionals we are."

She waited, watching the expressions twist and turn across Marsha's face. Then the woman relented, and her shoulders sagged. Sidney let her breath out slowly. It could've been so much worse.

Marsha looked up at her and gave her a small, fragile smile. "I'd like that. Have a nice evening." With one more smile, she turned and walked away.

Sidney fell back down in her chair and looked to Brock. "Oh, my God. That was hard."

He reached across the table, grabbed her hand and said, "It might've been hard, but you did a damned good job."

IN FACT, SIDNEY had done better than good. She had been professional, but easygoing, and somehow, she had taken Marsha's ire and turned it into something completely different. He knew in that moment, he should never have had any doubts. He hadn't really, but there always had been that question in his mind about whether she was right for him. Now he knew. There was no one more perfect for him, ever. Just that simple act of trying to make something of a relationship with Marsha made him love her all that much more.

It made him realize how hanging onto his own feelings of bitterness about his accident and the sense of defeat had hurt him. He hadn't actually seen Sidney's magic, but it had worked on him just as it had worked on Marsha. He felt whole again. He had let all that anger go, and he was so much better for it. He just hadn't understood how far he'd come, but now he did as he watched Marsha picking up coffee and dessert. Even her bearing was different now. She had a bounce in her step, a swing in her hips, a smile on her face.

That's how he felt—as if something inside had been settled, been resolved. It was put away in his past where it belonged. Dealt with, so he could move forward. With his own miracle—Sidney.

He stared down at his coffee cup, stunned by the realization. He had no idea his feelings were that deep, but they were. Like a slow river moving way below the earth. When they popped up, it was certainly a surprise. He had no doubt about the validity of the experience, the reality of his feelings. She was somebody he could really relate to. He wanted her like he'd never wanted another woman. She reached across and stroked his hand and said, "You're so quiet. Problems?"

He smiled into her eyes and said, "Yes."

She raised an eyebrow. "What's the problem?"

"You," he said with a smile. "I don't think I've ever met

anybody more admirable than you."

Clearly self-consciously pleased, she gave a laugh. "No, not true. This place is full of them." She motioned around them. "You're just looking through rose-colored glasses."

"No," he said with a smile. "I'm just now seeing the truth for what it really is."

She frowned, and he could see the little bit of worry coming into her gaze. Hell, he was feeling a little nervous and worried, himself.

"This is the truth, and I want you to be happy about it," he said. She was starting to push back, leaning against her chair. He knew she was doing what she usually did. When there was an unpleasant truth coming out, she was trying to step away. So it wouldn't hurt so much.

"Well, I hope you will," he said. "Because it's really something major."

She studied him and waited. He took a deep breath.

"I just realized how much I love you."

Tears came to her eyes. She reached across the table and grasped his hands in both of hers. "Maybe it's been really fast. Maybe you don't know really how you're feeling. Maybe it's more a case of being grateful you're healthy and strong now, and you can leave soon."

"Stop," he ordered. "I'm an adult. I have a very good idea of what I feel, how I feel, and why I feel this way. I understand you might be nervous, a little scared. But then, hell, so am I."

She stared at him, and then, in a small voice, she whispered, "Really? Do you?"

That note of vulnerability was his undoing. He picked up her hand, brought it to his lips and kissed it.

"Absolutely, I love you."

She leaned forward, her hand going on top of his. Although it seemed they were in a small, private bubble of their own, he knew that wasn't so. She'd gotten in enough trouble because of his actions.

Not anymore.

Then, she surprised him. She leaned forward, squeezing his hand, and said, "You'd better. You'd better be sure because I love you, too, and I don't think I could stand it if this was misplaced gratitude."

Not giving a damn if anyone saw them or not, he leaned across the table, tilted her chin and kissed her. He wanted the whole world to see. Wanted them to see she was his, and he was hers. Forever. When he slowly withdrew and leaned back in his chair, he said, "Convinced?"

A smile played out on the corner of her lips. "A little bit. Because that was just a *little bit* of a kiss."

He grinned boyishly. "Now, if we had the time and the opportunity, I could show you a whole lot more."

She smiled once again, tears coming to her eyes, and said, "I look forward to it." She stood, then he did, too. She threw herself into his arms.

"Dear God, I love you so much," she whispered. "I've never been happier."

His arms closed around her, and he knew exactly what she meant. Because neither had he.

Epilogue

The Next Day …

COLE SAT IN the wheelchair in the doorway to the dining area and studied his best friend. Brock had never looked happier. In fact, he couldn't imagine love sprouting from such a horrific event. There had been so little joy in Brock's life lately. Cole was really happy for him. It also gave him hope for himself. He'd been single for a long time. Of course, he'd been married before, then divorced. His being in the military had been brutal on his wife. She'd been terrified he would never come home. Finally, she couldn't stand living with it any longer. He'd understood, but it broke his heart. Five years later, he had a broken body to go with it.

He wondered if he was ever going to become whole again.

Brock had been filled with guilt and anger. But it looked like Sidney had a way about her because he was no longer the same bitter man Cole used to know. For that, he was grateful.

Maybe Hathaway House did perform miracles. He'd heard wonderful things about it before he'd applied for a transfer. Of course, his own arrival had been much less than stellar with him having to be transported right back to the hospital. But he was back now, and he was prepared for the fight of his life because he now saw hope in front of him. He saw a chance to become the man he had been.

Maybe not the exact same as he had been, because that likely wasn't possible, but he had a chance to become a man that was as good as he had been. Brock was living proof of that.

Cole wanted that for himself.

He hoped Hathaway House had just one more miracle to deliver. And if Cole was lucky, it had his name on it.

This concludes Book 2 of Hathaway House: Brock.

Read about Cole: Hathaway House, Book 3

Hathaway House: Cole (Book #3)

Welcome to Hathaway House. Rehab Center. Safe Haven. Second chance at life and love.

When Navy SEAL Cole Muster entered Hathaway House weeks ago, he was doing well. His meds were under control; his recovery was progressing at a safe rate, and he was getting better every day. But, left to his own devices, Cole pushed himself too hard and took himself off his medication—and ended up causing himself harm and earned himself time in a hospital. Now he's returned, hoping that Hathaway House can get him back on track one more time.

RN Sandra Denver feels responsible for what happened to Cole. She was his nurse and should have realized that he wasn't ready to leave Hathaway House. His setback was her fault, or at least she could have prevented it, if she'd made sure he was taking those meds she gave him daily. Now that he's back, she's finding it hard to trust not just him but herself. And she understands, when Cole has a hard time trusting himself too, it won't make his recovery any easier.

For Cole's sake, Sandra must help him overcome his stumbling blocks as well as her own. With any luck, they'll find a second chance at recovery, for both of them, at Hathaway House.

Book 3 is available now!

To find out more visit Dale Mayer's website.

http://smarturl.it/ColeDMUniversal

Author's Note

Thank you for reading Brock: Hathaway House, Book 2! If you enjoyed the book, please take a moment and leave a short review.

Dear reader,

I love to hear from readers, and you can contact me at my website: www.dalemayer.com or at my Facebook author page. To be informed of new releases and special offers, sign up for my newsletter or follow me on BookBub. And if you are interested in joining Dale Mayer's Reader Group, here is the Facebook sign up page.
facebook.com/groups/402384989872660

Cheers,
Dale Mayer

Get THREE Free Books Now!

Have you met the SEALS of Honor?

SEALs of Honor Books 1, 2, and 3. Follow the stories of brave, badass warriors who serve their country with honor and love their women to the limits of life and death.

Read Mason, Hawk, and Dane right now for FREE.

Go here and tell me where to send them!
http://smarturl.it/EthanBofB

About the Author

Dale Mayer is a USA Today bestselling author best known for her Psychic Visions and Family Blood Ties series. Her contemporary romances are raw and full of passion and emotion (Second Chances, SKIN), her thrillers will keep you guessing (By Death series), and her romantic comedies will keep you giggling (It's a Dog's Life and Charmin Marvin Romantic Comedy series).

She honors the stories that come to her – and some of them are crazy and break all the rules and cross multiple genres!

To go with her fiction, she also writes nonfiction in many different fields with books available on resume writing, companion gardening and the US mortgage system. She has recently published her Career Essentials Series. All her books are available in print and ebook format.

Connect with Dale Mayer Online

Dale's Website – www.dalemayer.com
Twitter – @DaleMayer
Facebook – dalemayer.com/fb
BookBub – bookbub.com/authors/dale-mayer

Also by Dale Mayer

Published Adult Books:

Hathaway House
Aaron, Book 1
Brock, Book 2
Cole, Book 3
Denton, Book 4
Elliot, Book 5
Finn, Book 6

The K9 Files
Ethan, Book 1
Pierce, Book 2
Zane, Book 3
Blaze, Book 4
Lucas, Book 5
Parker, Book 6
Carter, Book 7

Lovely Lethal Gardens
Arsenic in the Azaleas, Book 1
Bones in the Begonias, Book 2
Corpse in the Carnations, Book 3
Daggers in the Dahlias, Book 4
Evidence in the Echinacea, Book 5
Footprints in the Ferns, Book 6

Psychic Vision Series
Tuesday's Child
Hide 'n Go Seek
Maddy's Floor
Garden of Sorrow
Knock Knock…
Rare Find
Eyes to the Soul
Now You See Her
Shattered
Into the Abyss
Seeds of Malice
Eye of the Falcon
Itsy-Bitsy Spider
Unmasked
Deep Beneath
From the Ashes
Psychic Visions Books 1–3
Psychic Visions Books 4–6
Psychic Visions Books 7–9

By Death Series
Touched by Death
Haunted by Death
Chilled by Death
By Death Books 1–3

Broken Protocols – Romantic Comedy Series
Cat's Meow
Cat's Pajamas
Cat's Cradle
Cat's Claus
Broken Protocols 1-4

Broken and... Mending
Skin
Scars
Scales (of Justice)
Broken but... Mending 1-3

Glory
Genesis
Tori
Celeste
Glory Trilogy

Biker Blues
Morgan: Biker Blues, Volume 1
Cash: Biker Blues, Volume 2

SEALs of Honor
Mason: SEALs of Honor, Book 1
Hawk: SEALs of Honor, Book 2
Dane: SEALs of Honor, Book 3
Swede: SEALs of Honor, Book 4
Shadow: SEALs of Honor, Book 5
Cooper: SEALs of Honor, Book 6
Markus: SEALs of Honor, Book 7
Evan: SEALs of Honor, Book 8
Mason's Wish: SEALs of Honor, Book 9
Chase: SEALs of Honor, Book 10
Brett: SEALs of Honor, Book 11
Devlin: SEALs of Honor, Book 12
Easton: SEALs of Honor, Book 13
Ryder: SEALs of Honor, Book 14
Macklin: SEALs of Honor, Book 15
Corey: SEALs of Honor, Book 16

Warrick: SEALs of Honor, Book 17
Tanner: SEALs of Honor, Book 18
Jackson: SEALs of Honor, Book 19
Kanen: SEALs of Honor, Book 20
Nelson: SEALs of Honor, Book 21
SEALs of Honor, Books 1–3
SEALs of Honor, Books 4–6
SEALs of Honor, Books 7–10
SEALs of Honor, Books 11–13
SEALs of Honor, Books 14–16
SEALs of Honor, Books 17–19

Heroes for Hire
Levi's Legend: Heroes for Hire, Book 1
Stone's Surrender: Heroes for Hire, Book 2
Merk's Mistake: Heroes for Hire, Book 3
Rhodes's Reward: Heroes for Hire, Book 4
Flynn's Firecracker: Heroes for Hire, Book 5
Logan's Light: Heroes for Hire, Book 6
Harrison's Heart: Heroes for Hire, Book 7
Saul's Sweetheart: Heroes for Hire, Book 8
Dakota's Delight: Heroes for Hire, Book 9
Michael's Mercy (Part of Sleeper SEAL Series)
Tyson's Treasure: Heroes for Hire, Book 10
Jace's Jewel: Heroes for Hire, Book 11
Rory's Rose: Heroes for Hire, Book 12
Brandon's Bliss: Heroes for Hire, Book 13
Liam's Lily: Heroes for Hire, Book 14
North's Nikki: Heroes for Hire, Book 15
Anders's Angel: Heroes for Hire, Book 16
Reyes's Raina: Heroes for Hire, Book 17
Dezi's Diamond: Heroes for Hire, Book 18

Vince's Vixen: Heroes for Hire, Book 19
Heroes for Hire, Books 1–3
Heroes for Hire, Books 4–6
Heroes for Hire, Books 7–9
Heroes for Hire, Books 10–12
Heroes for Hire, Books 13–15

SEALs of Steel
Badger: SEALs of Steel, Book 1
Erick: SEALs of Steel, Book 2
Cade: SEALs of Steel, Book 3
Talon: SEALs of Steel, Book 4
Laszlo: SEALs of Steel, Book 5
Geir: SEALs of Steel, Book 6
Jager: SEALs of Steel, Book 7
The Final Reveal: SEALs of Steel, Book 8
SEALs of Steel, Books 1–4
SEALs of Steel, Books 5–8
SEALs of Steel, Books 1–8

Collections
Dare to Be You…
Dare to Love…
Dare to be Strong…
RomanceX3

Standalone Novellas
It's a Dog's Life
Riana's Revenge
Second Chances

Published Young Adult Books:

Family Blood Ties Series
Vampire in Denial
Vampire in Distress
Vampire in Design
Vampire in Deceit
Vampire in Defiance
Vampire in Conflict
Vampire in Chaos
Vampire in Crisis
Vampire in Control
Vampire in Charge
Family Blood Ties Set 1–3
Family Blood Ties Set 1–5
Family Blood Ties Set 4–6
Family Blood Ties Set 7–9
Sian's Solution, A Family Blood Ties Series Prequel
    Novelette

Design series
Dangerous Designs
Deadly Designs
Darkest Designs
Design Series Trilogy

Standalone
In Cassie's Corner
Gem Stone (a Gemma Stone Mystery)
Time Thieves

Published Non-Fiction Books:

Career Essentials

Career Essentials: The Résumé
Career Essentials: The Cover Letter
Career Essentials: The Interview
Career Essentials: 3 in 1